CLOUDS
ARE THE MOUNTAINS
OF THE WORLD

ALAN DAVIS

"Although these stories occur in many different parts of the country," Debra Marquart wrote of one of his books, "they are aesthetically shaped by the landscape of Louisiana, the muddy delta, and the oily bayou—the bottomland to which all things flow."

"I kept thinking that I wouldn't mind ending up as a character in one of his stories. Odds are, he'd do me justice." Dorothy Allison, *the New York Times Book Review*

"There is magic in a world that still somehow seems devoid of magic." *Publishers Weekly*

"Moving easily between blue-collar types and Social Register summer people, New Age dancers and Old World immigrants, underground poets and Elvis freaks, Davis demonstrates an impressive range in this collection." *Kirkus Reviews*

"A magical collection of stories, one of the best I've encountered in years. It's hard to convey my enthusiasm for this book—all the ordinary adjectives of praise seem trite and inadequate. But as personal testimony, I can say that I was tremendously moved and enlightened by each story, and that the collection as a whole lingers in my memory like a hometown—a place I once lived in and once loved." Tim O'Brien

CLOUDS
ARE THE MOUNTAINS
OF THE WORLD

ALAN DAVIS

woodhall press

Woodhall Press | Norwalk, CT

woodhall press

Woodhall Press, Norwalk, CT 06855
WoodhallPress.com
Copyright © 2024 Alan Davis

Cover design: LJ Mucci
Layout artist: LJ Mucci

Library of Congress Cataloging-in-Publication Data available

ISBN 978-1-960456-05-2   (paper: alk paper)
ISBN 978-1-960456-06-9   (electronic)

First Edition
Distributed by Independent Publishers Group
(800) 888-4741

Printed in the United States of America

Advance Comments

"This terrifying and comic novel-in-stories unfolds in the American heartland during a time—not many years hence—when the insurrectionists, militias, and purveyors of fake news have carried the day. Rule of law is a memory. Marauders roam the land, taking and raping at will. People live by their wits, and scruples are a luxury few can afford. The settings here are exotic, dangerous—burned-out towns, desert borderlands, highways that cut through depopulated prairie, communes controlled by sicko zealots, and the isolated forests of the Boundary Waters. The world Davis conjures is an existential horror, and yet his characters manage to find and create humanity and light. Three of them—a grandmother, daughter, and granddaughter—are the heroines whose resilience, love, and stoic humor give this book its narrative power and its shimmering, if tentative, offer of hope. *Clouds Are the Mountains of the World* is a compelling vision rendered in language, both surreal and chillingly familiar, that summons the apocalyptic dreams of Bruegel and Bosch."

—Lin Enger, author of *American Gospel, Undiscovered Country, The High Divide*

* * *

"What distinguishes Alan Davis's stark, beautifully written, postapocalyptic *Clouds Are the Mountains of the World* from other dystopian novels about a world gone to hell is its very ordinariness, its disconcerting banality. While Davis's vision of a post-Trump world does, indeed, include gun-toting bands of Marauders and Militias, corrupt Police and crazy radio talk-show hosts, a world of racism and economic and political chaos, they merely form the backdrop for humanity's real scourge—itself. Its selfishness, narcissism, irrational fear, tribalism, and, above all, mindless love of violence. In scene after scene in this novel-in-stories, we see what one of the main characters, Ava, says is the true problem: 'Hell is other people.' But the novel avoids cynicism and holds out that the only true hope for humanity is also people. Throughout we see the heroic quest of a family to reunite, despite the social upheaval and the daunting odds against them. Written in sparse, poetic prose, *Clouds* demonstrates that both our curse and our salvation lie within."

—Michael C. White, author of *Soul Catcher*, *A Brother's Blood*, and other novels

* * *

The characters in Alan Davis's *Clouds Are the Mountains of the World* are, like many of us, either afflicted by or surviving the impact of two lingering viruses—one of them biological, shared through spit and air, and the other a more insidious, contagious spread of small-minded and fearful ideals that breed violence, ignorance, and distrust. From the inside of a car to the inside of a suburban bubble to the inside of a dive bar, Davis's Midwesterners grapple with or have adapted, in their unique ways, to these destructive outside forces and carry on in their relentlessly, and sometimes absurdly, human ways that can also, despite their intentions, be beautiful. Nana, one of *Mountains'* recurring characters, at one point remembers a friend who died and was buried, and 'It gave her comfort to imagine blossoms growing out of his skull.' Davis's America of the future is like that skull: the remains of what was—and what will never be again. His characters are the blossoms growing out of it."

—Kris Tsetsi, author of *The Age of the Child* and *Pretty Much True*

"Between this earth and that sky I felt erased and blotted out."

—Willa Cather, *My Antonia*

* * *

"You are neither here nor there,
 a hurry through which known and
 strange things pass."

—Seamus Heaney

* * *

Build me a house near to the sea,
Build me a house that looks something like me.
Build me a house close to the water,
Build me a house that safeguards my daughter.

—Ava

Contents

To my wife Catherine; to my children Sara and Dillon (and his wife Gro Jeanett); and to my grandchildren Sienna, Beckett and Emrik.

And in memory of my brother Jimmy, 1951-2023.

PART ONE
The Dakotas

Fame is fleeting,
Life is short.
You take your beating
And you depart.

—Ava

This Earth, That Sky

The two Travelers—both women; one older, one young—together in a pickup with a camper shell where they sometimes slept.

They drove the rural and snow-spackled Dakotas toward the horizon on a wintry afternoon across flat farmland blanketed in snow under the threat of more weather. "Nana, those are mountains."

"Serena, those are clouds." Nana held tight to the wheel. She knew the tires on the truck were bald. When wind flared, old snow stippled the highway, obscuring it. Sometimes she felt the truck skid. Late afternoon shimmered, alive with breaking flocks of birds heading south.

"Nana, they're mountains."

"They look like mountains, don't they?"

She wouldn't argue, even in jest. A large flock of dark birds wheeled above them, fighting for purchase against harsh wind, finally admitting defeat and flying with the wind, unable to go south. A fly buzzed against the windshield until she opened her window and shooed it out.

"Shoo fly, shoo fly," Serena said, laughing.

A darkness was coming. It felt to Nana like vertigo, and she wondered if what she saw was shadows made by congealing jelly in the aging vitreous of her eyes. She shook her head to clear her vision. "Without clouds, the land in these parts would feel naked."

Serena narrowed her eyes to concentrate. "They don't just look like mountains; they are mountains." She had the open face of a young, bronzed angel, or what Nana imagined an angel would be if such things could light upon the uninhabitable parts of the Earth. At ten she had baby fat, despite their hit-and-miss diet, and fleshy fingers the color of hard-packed earth. She enjoyed making things, whether with thread or felt or colored pencil, and playing games of all kinds: board games with cards or dice and any other game found at a flea market or in one of the abandoned moldy aisles in the new ghost towns as the Dakotas emptied out. People died, moved on. There was nothing there anymore for anybody looking for a life. The ones who remained, who had connections, whether tribal or ancestral, sometimes stayed in place, locked and loaded. The others lived in the cities or close to the interstate highways, where Police still patrolled, at least during the day, when they kept a kind of order, the ones who could be trusted.

The two were on the run.

Nana sometimes found herself hobnobbing in the little shops in the inhabited towns that still speckled the land. She was social. She needed conversation. There wasn't much of that anymore. Her husband, Martin Gonzalez, had been shot dead by somebody they thought was a friend. It felt like medieval times. It was hard to know whom to trust. Shops in many towns were closed or had very limited hours. "OUT OF BUSINESS." How many times had they seen that sign hung from a doorway or painted on a window? "WHAT'S

LEFT IS YOURS," one said. That shop had been cleaned out long before they arrived.

They had stayed the previous night in an abandoned bed-and-breakfast called the Out-of-the-Way B&B, with Victorian lace doilies and a collection of bone china teacups on every available surface, all dusty and half broken, each with a gaily painted wooden troll inside. A single gleaming toaster on the breakfast buffet table actually worked, a piece of crumbled toast still in it. Dust covered everything. Nothing had been plundered, only broken. There was a frozen loaf of bread in the kitchen freezer.

Nana had dreamed that night of a man who took her ticket from her, the ticket that could get them into a room where nobody died. He held it before her but refused to punch it. "I paid for it," she argued. He stared stone-faced, like unyielding gneiss in a field, hate burning in his eyes as he put the ticket in his pocket and turned away.

The electricity still hummed in the house. It was a mystery. We could stay here a time, she thought, if it wasn't close to the highway. Not out-of-the-way enough.

"Nana," Serena said when the toast, frozen no more, popped up so fiercely that it sprung to the table and almost fell to the filthy floor, "that toast is ready, and it's not going to butter itself." There was no butter. She and Serena could kill whole weeks like that, traveling through towns where people once lived and thrived, stopping here and there, burning the days. Nana had a wad of money from the house she once owned and kept it in a compartment under the seat. She felt a catch in her throat. "The whole world given away for twenty-four pieces of silver," she muttered. The bitterness was like habanero, burning the tongue.

She knew they had to find a place to settle, a community to take them in, or try their luck in Fargo, where she and her daughter, with Martin, had once lived, and hope for the best. Traveling was a way to kill time. It was also a way to get killed. Stay in one place, everybody said. On the road, without a convoy, you're meat. And Nana had grown old for such a life. "They're mountains, Nana. I can see snow."

But she felt alive, safe on the road. Maybe it was disease after all the mayhem, a claustrophobia she couldn't quit without moving, but Serena deserved better.

In the car Nana reached and squeezed the young girl's arm. "We don't have mountains in this part of the world. The horizon is almost flat."

Alert, Serena turned toward her. "What's horizon?"

"It's where earth and sky appear to meet."

"Do they meet?" Serena studied the road. "It looks like it. But we never get there."

"No, they hope to meet but don't, just look like it. A tragic love story. Romeo and Juliet. Lancelot and Guinevere. Orpheus and Eurydice. Pocahontas and John Smith. Rama and Sita. Frieda and Diego Rivera."

"The Fantastic Four. The Black Panther," Serena added, smirking. "The Three Stooges."

"John and Yoko," Nana added. "Jimi Hendrix and the sky." She felt a catch in her throat. They were all dead. Was there anything that wasn't? "I barely remember," she said.

"They are so over, Nana."

"Why are they over?"

"Why don't we ever get there?"

"That's a very good question, Serena." She thought, *There's nowhere to get, that's why.* It was strange, how she felt safe on the road, in danger if cooped in a farmhouse with people they might trust or in a city where people might or might not give a shit. She remembered Martin Gonzalez. That had been more than a year ago. She was still a handsome woman, she knew that; but the last man she came across after Martin, who had been good, had wanted something from her but wouldn't give a thing in return. He had turned her to the ground

6

and taken her from behind but let her live. Serena had not been in the yard at the time, but it would have made no difference to him.

That would never happen again. She staked her life on it.

The road is better than the roadhouse. Live free or die. She liked the sound of that.

The two of us and nobody else. Nobody else in the world. The last two people on Earth, except for the caravans of homeless with haunted eyes and filthy faces they saw sometimes in a field camping for the night or driving ahead of them in battered vehicles that she would go out of her way to avoid. The military convoys, coming from someplace and going someplace else. The occasional farmer in a combine plowing the fields, often with a son or wife or friend standing guard, holding a rifle—the equivalent of a scarecrow meant as a warning not to birds but to people like her. "There's nothing for you here," the profile with its rifle said.

It was impossible to know how much of the contagion the land carried, so Nana had no interest in scavenging food from fields. Some people were still good. They would help an older woman and child, but she kept her foot on the accelerator. "We need gas," she said. "Goat Hollow is up ahead. The pumps there are still open, I've heard."

"Heard from who?"

"You know. Word gets around. The telephone telegraph. Things have changed; I don't know why, but we still find company, don't we? This is still adventure, isn't it?" The words rang hollow, but she repeated them anyway, for Serena.

"You don't know why?" The question was high-pitched. Nana could hear a twang in Serena's voice, anxiety rising. What were the rules of this game? Were they all of a sudden talking about something else?

"I have an idea, but I don't want to give you the wrong information. Why don't you pull out your crystal ball?" Serena had an old smartphone, which had long ago belonged to her mother, Ava, who was now (so far as Nana knew) so far away, up in the Boundary Waters, taken there by one of the men they were running from, who would find them if they stayed put, especially in Fargo, that she might as well be in another galaxy. Ava knew Serena had the phone, still with the same area code and number. Maybe one day she would call, Serena hoped, but Nana didn't think Ava would be heard from again. Not in her lifetime, anyway.

Sometimes the phone brought them news. It was useful to know where the bands of Marauders were last seen. Law enforcement had mostly abandoned the Dakotas to the Militias, and word of mouth was essential, but the interstates and cell towers were still patrolled and protected. What good that would do on a lonely stretch, she couldn't say. The phone was the most precious thing Serena owned, because it came from her mother and put her in touch with the world. It also gave her something to do. The world inside the phone often—too often, Nana thought—absorbed her attention, so that the world—the real world, Nana thought—vanished. As the Dakotas emptied out, the virtual world blinked on and off too.

There were no guarantees anymore. Had there ever been?

"Will we ever reach the horizon, Nana?"

"No. It's like tomorrow. We never get there. We wake up and it's today."

"Nana, we do get there. Tomorrow we'll be there." Serena had the white, burnished phone with a cracked screen in her lap. Nana noticed a black SUV approaching fast behind them. There was a rumble in the sky, the sound of fighter planes flashing past, the supersonic boom of one breaking the speed of sound. Had the country's Dear Leader started another war to divert attention from the chaos everywhere? She couldn't keep up anymore.

"We need gas," Nana said. The gauge was close to empty.

"Won't we get there tomorrow?"

"Tomorrow when you say "tomorrow," you won't mean the same day that you mean right now when you say that word. Get it? We can't step in the same river twice because the water in it isn't the same water that was there the first time we got our toes wet." Nana found her mind perambulating from where she was and into the kind of trance that lets a driver go for miles lost in the *thunk-a-thunk* of tires *kalunk*-ing over seams in the asphalt. The gas gauge was in the red zone. The last three stations had been closed. For good. One had been ransacked, the attached convenience store's picture window shattered and shelves emptied. She could feel tears well up and fought them back. It wouldn't do to weep. Not in front of Serena.

The black SUV had tinted windows and was riding their back fender. Nana snapped her fingers. It was a sign. Serena stopped talking and reached to open the glove compartment. The muscles in her wrists straining, she took out the heavy pistol, keeping the barrel pointed away from them both, unclicked the safety, and passed it to Nana, who placed it snug in her lap.

The tension in the car didn't break until the SUV swung into the passing lane and held steady beside them, a passenger with aviator glasses staring at her with such intensity that she showed him the gun. Nana saw white teeth before the passenger turned to the driver and the SUV roared past. She slowed to increase the distance between them. Soon enough it had disappeared into the horizon they never reached.

She handed the gun, safety engaged again, to Serena, who put it back into its compartment and played with her phone. "I found a site where they say the horizon is a question of perspective."

It took Nana more than a moment to come back. "That's right. Things look smaller when they're far away. That's perspective." Though she kept the thought to herself, she was surprised the AI voice on the phone still functioned as normally as it did. Parts of the world still worked. The cell towers and relays, some of them, were still up. The Police protected technology more than people. Fargo might be safer than the road.

9

"Hmm. Sometimes they're not that much bigger when you get close," Serena said. Nana could hear dread in her voice. A panic attack—something new this week, but frequent in their picaresque life—itched to get loose. "Why can't we ever get there?"

Uh-oh. She could tell that Serena might whine, then complain, which could become a tantrum, or worse. It could get so bad that it might crash the system until there was nothing to do but stop the car and wait it out. "We're getting closer. It doesn't seem like it because the landscape looks the same on both sides of the road as far ahead as we can see, all that dirty snow, the swirl of the wind on the road, but trust me." *Trust me*, she thought, almost desperate. She could smell her stale stink, the funk of dread and fear. She needed a shower. "Soon enough we'll be there, even though it feels like we never get any closer to where we want to be." And where the hell exactly was that?

That was the question. To be or not to be?

To be, to be, to be, she thought.

A great sadness clouded her vision, like a mystic's dream of peace destroyed by a false idol. "Your mother will find us, or we'll find her." She could see Ava, her daughter, as brave or braver than Serena, until the dope sickness took hold and congealed her life into tilting desire for the next fix.

It didn't really matter anymore what Nana said to Serena. It was all BS.

It was past time to leave the Dakotas for good, just like so many others had done. Get down to Tulsa, the land of tornadoes, where it was supposed to be safe, where civilization was still intact, where people were welcome, more than welcome, or so she had heard, but that would be one long, white-knuckled drive, and she found herself hoping that Ava would find them first. Otherwise, they needed to join a convoy; Nana didn't have the resources or skills to turn the tables and go find Ava, not up in the Boundary Waters.

They waited for the phone to ring but it never did, at least not with Ava's voice.

"We're not getting closer, Nana!" It sounded like a shriek; Serena had one hand tight around the phone. "It's farther away! Nana! I want to be there! Stop the car!" There was panic in her voice. "Where are we?"

"I want to be there too," Nana said, perversely stomping on the accelerator to tend to her own anxiety, glancing at the gas gauge, feeling her throat tighten, her own small hairball of panic finding purchase. She opened the window to clear the air and saw the exit for Goat Hollow, which was on a promontory, not in a hollow, and didn't have any goats. It overlooked a lake with vacation houses around it, now mostly abandoned. "Goat Hollow will never lose its charm," she remembered a friend, a historian of the region, telling her once. He was dead now. The Marauders had come through like a sky filled with locusts and left death and devastation behind. They had beaten him to death when he told them to get the hell out of town; he had always been a man who had no filters. That was what she had heard, anyway, that he was dead and gone, like an old blues song. He had been buried in a field of flowers. It gave her comfort to imagine blossoms growing out of his skull.

The gas station had survived, maybe bought safety with fuel. She hoped it was still open. We aren't helpless, she told herself, and repeated the sentence like a mantra. Resist. Fight back. Prevail.

Snow swirled on the blacktop and made driving difficult. Serena's phone pinged, a message from somebody better placed in the world, and she started thumb texting. She was very good at it. She had text pals all over the world, but not in the Dakotas. They gave her hope that something better was ahead, over the horizon.

The panic that had been with them in the car like a crow keening over carrion took a break. She rolled the window back up. Thank God for attention deficit, Nana thought. Her own mind went traveling, far away from the narrow, deserted road with loose snow swirling across it. She remembered a picnic in a state park where the land was so desolate that it was beautiful, awe-inspiring. The weather dropped almost 30 degrees in a matter of hours; feeling it happen was life-altering. Her mother had been there, her father, her sister, her daughter, and an infant: Serena.

She rested in the memory. The panic passed. So many no longer alive upon the Earth. But isn't that the way it always is—generations flipping like decks of playing cards in the hands of a gambler? Everything was broken, but nothing had changed. The first rule of life is that everything dies. Maybe not so fast, though, maybe not so quick.

She drove along two-lane blacktop. Goat Hollow was twelve miles away. One section of road with shelter belts of bare-limbed trees on either side had mounds of snow rising up and tilting toward them. Somebody was keeping the road open with a plow. The invisible hand of civilization still had its story to tell.

"Nana?"

The word took her by surprise. "Yes, Serena?"

"Are you crying?"

"Crying? No, I—yes, yes, I guess I am. Funny how that can happen."

"Why are you crying?"

"Why? About something that happened in somebody else's life that I can't do anything to make better."

"Really? There's no medicine?"

"No, there isn't." She thought about it and slowed when she felt the tires slide into roadside gravel. The truck with its bare tires could be a boat, she thought, sailing across a great sea of white foam. "Well, there might be medicine, but it doesn't work." Not anymore, she thought. Too many quacks and con men. She waited for her own phone in her pocket to ping. Somebody would contact her. There had to be someplace in the Dakotas that was still safe, where "solitary" was a catchword and not a nightmare. She could remember not so long

12

ago driving over a cattle guard to spend three nights with a family of farmers she had met in better times. They had made their money from oil. The land was spoiled, but they had built a sanctuary. They grew food in greenhouses even in winter.

Two cowboys had stood on either side of the cattle guard and given the stink eye to her and the child. "Hey, honey," one said. She had showed him the gun. He had raised his hands like a marionette in an exaggerated shrug to show there would be no trouble. "Crazy bitch," he muttered.

The farm family was alarmed to hear about it, because they didn't know the cowboys. But at least they were just aimless drifters, not Marauders, and the family had fed the girl and the woman well; shared what they knew about conditions, particularly on the coast, where the waters were so high that some cities had built walls that didn't do much good; and packaged up some food for them. They even tried—half-heartedly—to convince them to stay. "Thanks, many thanks," she said. They headed back to the interstate and drove some days, stayed put on others, but never traveled, if they could help it, after dark.

"Medicine won't help? It's not that kind of predicament?" Serena asked. Nana was surprised she knew the word. Maybe it was something she had heard on one of the podcasts she subscribed to. Nana thought of the podcasts as little DNA packets of mediated information that might or might not be true about everything under the sun. "How about hugs and kisses, Nana? That always helps, doesn't it? *Mamá* always told me that."

"That almost always helps, doesn't it?" she said, half listening, pre-occupied. "But in this case I don't think it can do much good." She scanned the roadside for temporary shelter, someplace they could hide if the need arose. There were farm roads, driveways, places to stop and hole up and sleep if need be in the shelter of the truck's camper shell. Even a grove of trees might do the trick if they could get to it from the blacktop in the snow. She had rope and cowbells she placed around the truck to tip them off if somebody with ill intentions entered their private space. Sometimes just the wind made a racket.

"Why not?" Serena laid the phone between her legs and turned toward her, now all ears. My granddaughter is well-made, Nana thought, a notion that threatened more tears. Minutes ago, she was close to panic. Now she's taking a considered view of things.

"I'm sorry to say this, Serena, but it's hard to explain to you." What's the right amount of information to share with a ten-year-old in such times?

"Will it make you cry again?"

Nana raised an eyebrow. What a clever thing to say. She considered the question. "It might. Even thinking about it makes me cry. But it's also something that 'will be easier to tell you about when you get a little bit older."

"When I reach the horizon, you mean?"

"It's about missing people and knowing what you would do if it was you inside their skin. And you love them, so much, but maybe they try to do what they think you want them to do instead of what they want to do themselves, or maybe they just don't know what they want. Things break, is what I'm trying to say. Things break inside people all over the world, and the world itself breaks, real bad, but I'm also making a mountain of a molehill because she's alive, I think, just not happy or able to make her life move ahead. As long as you're alive, there's hope."

"Who's her? And how do you know she's alive?"

"Let's not get into it."

"Somebody who might not come back? Somebody who doesn't give"—Serena made sure to emphasize, like a headmistress, each of the next four words—"a good god damn?" The car became quiet. Nana almost turned on the radio to break the tension. "I think I know."

"Okey dokey; maybe you do, but let's not get into it."

"Nana, you're crying again."

"Am I? That's okay. It's okay to cry." It's not, she thought, not now. "Just give me a minute." The clouds cleared ahead, on the horizon. Flakes of snow, portending worse weather, followed behind. It would be close to a full moon. Even with the sparse white flakes, both grandmother and granddaughter could see sun and moon like low-hanging fruit. A welcome oddity, but neither said a thing.

They reached Goat Hollow. It was a town that had seen better days. She could see the gas station down the road past a pawnshop with heavy bars across its front window and an antiques store with plywood instead of glass. Still, whatever the Marauders had wrecked, if that story was true, the town had cleaned up some.

Without being told, Serena retrieved the gun but didn't pass it to Nana, who could puncture an empty tin can smack dab in its middle from a distance of fifteen feet. She oiled it, kept it clean. Her father had liked guns and taught her what he could. Nana had done the same for Serena, but glanced at her in annoyance. "Let me have it," she said.

"No," Serena said. "I've got this." She sounded to Nana like a stone-cold killer.

The streets were empty. Snow crunched under the truck's wheels. Wind whistled in a minor key. The gas station was on a corner downtown, surrounded by brick buildings—a storefront black with soot and clearly vandalized, a few still looking sturdy and complete. This was a town that was still lived in.

An old white man with liver spots like creosote marks on his face and an oversized plaid shirt rolled up to the elbows that hid all but the bottom of his waistband holster emerged from the barred door of the station. He held out a palm like a traffic cop to indicate that she should stay inside the truck.

"Nana," Serena said, almost laughing, pointing. "Look. A troll!"

Nana grinned hard to keep a straight face and retrieved a face mask—it didn't pay to be careless these days—some cash from her purse, unrolled the window, and showed it to the owner. Walking hunched like a crab, he approached the cab cautiously. "Hiya," she said.

"Bad storm coming," he answered. She could see him take in the gun that her granddaughter held. "Why the mask?"

"Why not?" Nana said. "I don't know what's running its course in your town."

He grudgingly offered a cramped smile. "Why not Minot? Ha!" he said, about as fake a sound as she had ever heard. He took her money. He fiddled with her gas cap and the machine pumped. She watched the gauge on the pump to make certain they got their money's worth. "Receipt?" he asked, coming close to the window. He hacked out some phlegm. She could smell his breath despite the mask. Nicotine. Pork and beans. Whiskey.

She laughed. "Any food inside?"

He took a deep breath, seeming to consider the question. "Too late for the hot dish," he said. "Sorry about that."

She nodded. "Okay, then. I better let you go. Thank you."

He stood close. "Got a cot, though. For the night." He put one mottled hand on the windowsill. He opened his mouth. She thought he meant it as a smile. It came out a leer. She shook her head, took a glance at Serena. Let down her guard.

It happened fast. He leaned inside the truck as much as he could, the arm and his face, shouted in her ear something insane, and reached across her for the gun. Serena had both hands on its barrel, clenched it tight, and leaned as far from him as she could get. He did his best to wrench it from her, but couldn't quite reach it. His hand pawed empty air like a claw.

Nana clenched her other hand, the one close to the window, into a fist and drove her knuckles hard into the sagging jowls of the guy's chin with all her strength. He grunted, hacked. Lost his breath. Stepped back just long enough to give Serena time to get her trigger finger in place and raise it in his direction.

He put up his hands as if under arrest and backed a step away from the truck. "No problem," he said.

Serena kept the gun pointed his way. "Bad move, Buster," she said, as calm as Nana, who ached to take the weapon from her. "Don't be stupid."

"Don't be stupid," Nana said. She could see hate in his eyes.

"Bitch," he said. "Just want a good time. You got to be lonely for it too." He murmured something in a voice he must have thought was sweet and seductive and leaned toward her again.

She stared at him, dumbfounded. "What part of 'Don't be stupid' don't you understand? Back away."

The man's hand reached under his plaid shirt. He got his pistol out of its holster. He was slow, though, as if the thing weighed more than he expected. Serena, holding her own gun steady, setting it up with both hands the way Nana had taught her, shot him twice, once in the chest and a second time higher up in the forehead when the gun kicked.

"We got him!" she shouted. "Got him, Nana!" Without thinking she gave the weapon to her grandmother, whose ears were ringing so awful that she was deaf. "Bull's-eye!" Serena shouted. "Bull's-eye!"

Her eyes gleamed manic.

The guy lay twitching on the cracked concrete beside the car like a wounded deer next to the roadway, his arms splayed out on either side of him, his eyes wide, the smell of gun smoke filling the cab. Nana tried to catch her breath. Her ears rang. She was shaking, but she started up the truck. She kept it in park. Pointing the gun toward the body, now lying still in a growing mess of blood, she stepped out, leaving open the truck's door, and kicked away his weapon. She bent down and laid a finger across the inside of one of his wrists. She still had the shakes. There was no pulse. She reached in a pocket of his plaid shirt and took back her money, stared past the pumps into the dark inside of his office.

"Nana!" Serena shouted loud enough for her to hear. It shocked away her trance. "Let's vamoose!" It was still a game to Serena, high as a kite on adrenaline. It would be a hard night when it faded and the shakes paid a visit.

Nana grabbed the man's gun and hopped into the truck.

She stared into the rearview mirror as she pulled into the street. Main Street was quiet. Nobody in sight. As they drove, she said anything that popped into her head. "No more gas from Goat Hollow." She babbled nonsense. Her head felt stretched, as if her brainpan dripped oil. The tinnitus in her ears sounded like a loud bell that wouldn't stop ringing.

Serena shivered too, the way one person's yawn can be contagious, and smiled. "Nana," she said, a slur in her voice as if drunk, "it had to happen sooner or later. Now I don't have to guess what it's like." She smiled. "It felt good, Nana. It felt good to me. We had to do it, Nana, didn't we? We had to do it. We had no choice!"

She said it like a squawk. Nana heard that much, at least, though she could barely make out the words through the ringing in her ears. It was an astonishing thing for a ten-year-old to say.

"It was him or us, Nana. That troll got exactly what he deserved."

"He dealt the play," Nana agreed, remembering a phrase from a book. "You did what you had to do. He dealt the play." She felt the shakes coming on and thought she might have to stop driving, but she knew distance from Goat Hollow was their best friend. "I'm proud of you. Very proud."

"Kill or be killed, Nana," Serena said with pride. She had already regained equilibrium. It seemed impossible. Either that or she was quietly hysterical.

Was that it, then? The future? Kids with guns and sharp swords?

The two of them shouted out whatever came to mind—a call and response that kept them high, like sports fans shouting out cheers with energy that ebbed fast, at least for Nana, until they reached the interstate. Dread traveled with her, a companion she wanted to acknowledge but didn't. So did a fly. It buzzed in the car and couldn't be caught.

"Shoo fly," Serena shouted. She swatted at it and laughed maniacally. "Nana," she said, almost unable to speak through her laughter, "what's good for the goose" . . . her laughter came like a cascade of gelatinous oil dripping from a crankshaft every time she tried to continue. . . "Nana, what's good for the goose is good for the baba ghanoush!" She repeated the sentence in full a dozen times, cackling with each performance. It had been made famous by two standup comics in Fargo who called themselves Frankenstein and Faust. Nana hadn't realized Serena had ever heard the phrase, or of them. Life goes on.

There was no going back. Nana understood that. It was Serena's first kill.

When they had sobered up, when they settled somewhere for the night, the day's kill impossible to erase, there might be wailing, there might be the gnashing of teeth. Surely what had happened so quickly would return, a haunting, to fill her granddaughter with dark knowledge.

Or could she put it aside the ways kids do? Was that the way it was now?

Nana, though she could still hear the gunshots, smell the singe of powder in the car, was already working on the problem. A silence came between them. Nana felt inner darkness enshroud her like sticky humidity on a muggy day. *It is what it is*, she thought, a sentence so completely empty of meaning that it gave her comfort.

"Why can we see the moon during the day?" Serena said, back to herself. It sounded unreal. From a cold-blooded defender of womanhood to a confused child at the speed of light. "Does that mean something's wrong with the sky? Tell me, Nana. Tell me!"

The sun was dim, the moon visible in daylight. An odd sight. A comfort.

"It's a children's moon," Nana said.

Serena, relieved that there was an answer at hand, offered a puzzled look. "You mean like a naked moon?"

She had already put behind her, at least for the moment, what she had done. And the emotional consequences, Nana reminded herself, to kill a person and not reduce them in memory to nothing but scum. Just a sign of the times, maybe. *We'll talk that out later.* For now, she was just grateful she could hear again. "It's called that because in the old days kids couldn't stay up nights to study the moon. This one, though, it's there for all to see." Nana's mood lifted. "Emotions are like clouds," she said. "If you wait them out—" She stopped speaking, catching up with herself. The fly buzzed again in the car, or was that the tinnitus after the gunshots?

Serena swatted at it. Nana opened the front windows and a cold, bracing wind blew through the compartment.

"Is it gone?" Nana said. "Did we get it?"

"A fly in the ointment," Serena said. She giggled and couldn't stop. "A fly! In the ointment!"

Nana buzzed up the windows and thought with an ache of Ava, her daughter, Serena's mother, who had grown ferociously angry at what the world had become; at what men did to women, to the land, to each other. For Ava it was all savagery and anger and addiction. Butchery, treachery. Save us from sickness, Nana thought, from accidents, from addictions. Protect us from the longing we have to damage ourselves.

Her own first husband had been a drunk and child beater. Dead now. Good riddance. At least I had some time with Martin. He was a good man. Something to remember aside from the wars, the Marauders and Militias, the plagues, the rising seas, the mass migrations, the pandemics that found their way from birds to pigs to humans.

Nana felt her rage rise. All brought about by men. Her granddaughter had shot a man dead, done what had to be done. That couldn't be taken back, but in a hundred years, who would care? Women do things too—to other women, to children, and of course to men—but it's men who attack and attack and attack. The one who had taken Ava, who wanted Serena alive because she was worth good money if he could make her grandmother dead. Where was he? Where was Ava? Was she still in his clutches?

She drove. And remembered Martin Gonzalez. He had been a good man.

Maybe it was time to stop waiting for Ava and leave the Dakotas for good, see if Tulsa was safe like they said. Big stone buildings with Art Deco swirls on them and a police force that protects and serves, rumor had it. What a novelty that would be. She liked the sound of the word: "Tulsa."

Clouds were visible again on the horizon. Serena no longer insisted that they were mountains, but Nana saw a house on a rocky promontory, a trick of the waning light.

If clouds were mountains, they could be in the Rockies, surrounded by stone that would keep them safe, in a cabin with oak doors and thick forest all around them. She saw a big, naked tree held fast by its roots in the middle of a faraway, stubbled field. "We're like that tree," she said, "except it's rooted in one place, a part of everything, and for some reason we can't stop. We have to keep going."

To nowhere, she thought, remembering the lyrics of a long-ago song. I could stand there naked, she thought, in one of those distant windows, in that imposing mansion, inside a mirage. I could stand there, not like an exhibitionist, longing for attention, making a statement, protesting so much merde, but simply to say, "Here I am. I stand here naked in my chrysalis; make of it what you will."

"Whatever," Serena said, as if it explained everything, and maybe it did. "Whatever." She shrugged and stared toward the horizon until the highway angled away from the children's moon. "Nana? You listening?"

"Yeah," she said. "I am. Whatever. It is what it is."

They drove under the moon, now covered by clouds that still looked like mountains. Snow. It was a cold place much of the year, always had been. That would never change. Things might be different in Tulsa.

They could see the horizon.

Would they ever reach it?

The Cafeteria Strut

Chuck Larson, all-state in three sports but particularly potent on the football field, was the most popular boy in high school despite his guess in History that the Rosetta Stone was a ski mountain in Colorado. He was so popular girls actually fainted—this is no joke—at the sight of him each day as he strutted from the gym after practice to the cafeteria with Coach at his side and a phalanx of back-seat buddies and beefy linemen. Coach had his table tennis paddle with him so that he could whack anybody who didn't hustle. When Chuck and his entourage reached the cafeteria, carefully trained food service personnel served them a special gourmet meal, food and service the rest of us couldn't buy even at Famous Dave's Bar-B-Que. If we had tuna fish, for Chuck and his cronies it was steak and walleye. If we had hamburger stretched with soybeans, for Chuck it was a fifty-four-ounce tomahawk ribeye.

Those were simple times. All of us felt safe inside whatever cocoon we happened to inhabit. Except for me. Or that's how I felt, anyway, as if I was alone and hung out to dry in the teeter-totter world that went bad. Chuck bathed in adulation the way a voluptuary samples powders and perfumes, seldom so ravenous that he didn't take a good twenty minutes to strut to the cafeteria. He soaked up glory like a sponge. By the time he became a senior with two Dakota state championships under his belt, the fainting girls were a problem. Coach recruited several misfits like myself to sit on benches at strategic points on the cafeteria route. "Do a bang-up job," Coach said, tapping his paddle against one humongous thigh, "and I won't run the hell out of you." Coach was famous for those fifty-minute runs. He would take us outside and sit himself down in a lawn chair that sagged under his weight. He would place his paddle on one thigh, take out his stopwatch, and shout, "Go"!"

We went. It was good training for life's hard knocks, he liked to say. "When you go out in the world," he said, "you'll need a pistol in one pocket and brass knuckles on almost every finger."

Sad thing is, he turned out to be something like right.

We were supposed to protect the fainting girls from bruises, concussions, and an unladylike disarray of clothing when they keeled over. The job was a privilege, Coach told us, and he would see to it that we were recognized at the year's last pep rally. "Chuck himself will give you a salute," Coach said in a high nasal voice that sounded almost feminine, the result of a near-fatal accident. Maxwell, the misfit who took credit for the accident, loved to parody Coach's reedy voice. Before Coach dismissed us, he told us we would have to bring our lunches and stay to the sidewalk benches we were assigned. "Chuck doesn't like to see the girls get hurt."

"If he doesn't do right by us," Maxwell said to me, "I'll start pounding nails into his footprints again. Maybe a spear in the pipes wasn't enough for the old geezer, huh?" Maxwell was a gamer. He believed in magic.

I shrugged. One must fasten one's gaze, I thought—something I'd read in a book and taken to heart. I lived on the bench anyway, staring at the water tower across campus that glinted in the bright sun, the same tower I could see from the rented house where I lived with my sick mother and my father, a trucker who was seldom at home, which was a good thing. When he was in the house, things went to hell in a handbasket. As I waited for a glimpse of Molly, the girl I loved hopelessly, it was easy to pretend that the water tower really was the Rosetta Stone and that Chuck flew down its hieroglyphic slopes in a hooded red parka, studying the terrain below with glances through a pair of sleek goggles. As for Molly, I was too bashful to speak to her, but I knew her schedule. She had pep squad when Chuck practiced, and I would see her jog to the gym in khaki shorts and top, stopping at the tall door to leap, one hand stretched high and her caramel-colored hair, if unbraided, flying every which way as a finger touched the head of the door with grace and triumph.

Maxwell was assigned the bench closest to the gym; it was his job to report the first sighting each day. Maxwell sometimes spent his free time creeping around campus with a silver ball-peen hammer in his book bag to pound fourpenny nails into Coach's footprints. He had learned in Anthropology that one tribe believed that such a ritual cursed the victim with impotence or caused some unpredictable tragedy to occur. When he wasn't stalking Coach with his silver hammer, his idea of a good joke was to tiptoe up to you while you daydreamed and squirt a mouthful of water in your ear.

His vendetta against Coach dated back to the day he spit, on a dare, into the face of a jock strutting toward him who said something demeaning to him. The jock, instead of beating him to a bloody pulp then and there and maybe getting suspended, dragged him to Coach, who was also the school's drama director and unofficial disciplinarian. The jock, aching for revenge, threw Maxwell down like a sack of potatoes on the proscenium as Coach worked in despair with the homecoming queen, or the HQ as we called her.

The HQ, whose name was Tina and who later came to a tragic end, was trying without much luck to learn her lines in *A Streetcar Named Desire*, a play chosen only because she and Chuck had seen the movie in a film class together and decided they had to play Blanche and Stanley. It would be a hoot, they thought, but the HQ had trouble remembering what time of the month it was, much less her lines. She was an atrocious actress even by the standards of Coach, whose idea of great drama were the television reruns of a sitcom called *Father Knows Best*. In need of a break, he opened his mouth into a broad smile and left the HQ to her own mnemonic devices. He nodded to the jock, who dragged Maxwell across a baseball diamond and two football fields to the school's septic tank.

Maxwell fought like hell, kicking and screaming. "You fuckface! Your fate is sealed!" That didn't deter the jock, his facial muscles as tight as a drum. He pulled Maxwell up the tank's metal ladder, rung by rung, with Coach urging him onward. The way Maxwell told it, Coach had a rubber-duckie smile the whole time that would have wiped clean a filthy latrine, but moments before the jock drowned him like the runt in a litter of kittens, Coach benevolently interceded. Instead of a dunking, Maxwell received the paddling of his young life. Coach saved him from what would have been a possibly terminal dunking, but also earned his undying animus.

Each day after our new assignment, which, absurd as it was, was sanctioned by the school's principal, Maxwell took a bologna sandwich and two checkered flags to a perch near the gym. The rest of us, tense, nervous, sat on other benches farther along the school's covered walk, quickly dispatching our own gummy cheese sandwiches as we waited for Chuck. Maxwell was supposed to follow Chuck like a familiar. If there was an early flurry of fainting, we expected him to wave the flags like a switchman, but he was unreliable.

Sometimes he gave greater priority to his lunch than to the protection of delicate female skulls. They fell like tenpins. At other times he waved the black-and-white flags like an artist covering airy canvas with fluid swirls of checkered cloth, hypnotizing himself, working off adrenaline and anger, oblivious to our confusion.

We hated Coach too, but at least we got the chance to cradle fainting coeds. Maxwell had only the taste of bologna on his breath and, for company, only his checkered flags, his silver hammer, and his fourpenny nails.

The girls would synchronize their watches during morning announcements and gather near noon in sleek coteries along the covered walk. Without Maxwell's flags to warn us, they sometimes fell like glass trinkets, eyes rolling back as though watching themselves faint. "Is he hot or what?" we heard them say, which was often fair warning. It was a form of sexual hysteria that I had never witnessed before. It required adolescents of a certain age with overactive metabolisms and imaginations to drop as if shot through the head at the sight of a muscular, hormone-crazed young man. One of them, Dee Dee—an airhead if ever there was one—followed him everywhere with such devotion that she became a bad joke, though she was nice to me; and later, when I heard that she ended up in prison after a bizarre accident that killed a man, I was sorry I hadn't tried to help her before she went completely off the rails.

From my bench I would stare down the walkway, dazzled by the carnival of swirling color. Their suntanned legs were more suitable for bareback riding over ranchland than for restless drumming beneath desks smudged with inky fingerprints and carved with graffiti. The most provocative girls had permanents or carefully styled bouffants, a sight seldom seen anymore except in old movies or TV series set in the middle of the last century. We lived in an alternate universe. They wore short skirts and stood on heels, hips cocked. Almost without exception, rumor had them available for more than malted milks if you were Chuck or one of the anointed members of his offensive line. The linemen favored long, thick mullets that year. Some things never change.

A few of the girls were more modest, more ladylike, at least until Chuck arrived. They would lean toward Chuck like long-stemmed flowers, their faces clear with health or the miracles of dermatology. Once, I passed Molly in the doorway of the Social Science building, her hair braided and her eyes full of sparkles of light as Chuck flirted with her. He winked at me. "You a freshman?"

I blushed, my mind paralyzed by his attention, until Molly slapped him playfully on the shoulder. "Hush, sweetie," she said. "He's a senior, same as us. Name of Heimlich." She pronounced it as Heimlich, with a "k" at the end, as if my mission in life was to apply pressure on the abdomen between the naval and the rib cage.

"Heimlich?" Chuck said, grinning his infamous good-natured, shit-eating grin. "Is that maneuver named after you?"

But Chuck was more than just a senior. Robust and good-looking like some muscle-bound steroid freak, with high cheekbones and a square jaw, he always focused his eyes modestly on the middle distance. In *Streetcar* he flaunted his stuff, as though going all the way for a score, improvising like a pro when the HQ fainted on stage after he removed his shirt and thumped his chest. He stayed in character and carried her to the wings. While Coach revived her with smelling salts, Chuck put his shirt back on and returned with her understudy. Everyone except the stage technicians, like me, backstage, hooted and hollered and thought the fainting spell was part of the script.

The day after this performance, the campus was abuzz. "Oh, my God; is he hot or what? Oh, my God!" the girls murmured. Dee Dee, one of the high-maintenance girls, had fainted more than a dozen times. Like Tina, she too came to a bad end later when she got a guy's head stuck in her car's windshield, which is a story for another time, but that day she was high only on Chuck.

Coach expected an epidemic of fainting. He spoke to us briefly in the well-modulated tones of a snake oil salesman, invoking the saintly power of positive thinking. Then he waved his paddle in our

28

faces, reminding us that this was one day when mistakes would not be tolerated. Finally, he armed us with a medical device purchased through the generosity of an anonymous donor, "a philanthropist from over in Bismarck."

We pocketed these devices and hastened to our posts, behind and slightly to the side of whichever girl we had been selected to protect.

As luck would have it, I was assigned to Molly. She was one of the few girls who had never fainted, but I had studied her habits for so long that I was certain I would be able to predict when the amount of blood reaching her brain was no longer sufficient to compensate for the sight of Chuck. Then I would have three options: I could use my medical device, cushion her slow-motion tumble, or miss her and let her smack her skull as a way to hurt what I loved most.

In those days my empathy was limited. I imagined Molly would faint the way an alcoholic might pass out after one too many shots of rye. The sight of Chuck made girls about his age drunk, and I don't just mean Dee Dee; I mean girls I couldn't get out of my head. I was jealous of Chuck to beat the band. Those young women stared at him, their breathing grew short and heavy, some kind of sigh or grunt involuntarily escaping from their mouths, and they swooned to the ground like flowers that wilt after too much sun and rain.

Chuck knew what was waiting for him, of course, and he loved it. Unless he was especially hungry or running late, he took his time, loitering with each group of admirers, and the day after *Streetcar* would certainly be no exception. It was hard on all of us. I feared his occasional outbursts, but at least they were quick and merciful. He would emerge from the gym ravenous, crouched low, his steel-trap muscles rippling as he sprinted in a dazzle of broken-field running, bowling over any moving object without a skirt or faculty badge. The girls, bedazzled by such power, dropped like ticks pinched off the skin. Our low-budget reflexes were no match for such a blitzkrieg. On such days, Chuck seemed like perfection itself.

In fact, he only made one public mistake in his high school career; that near-fatal blunder, though nobody else knew it, was brought on by Maxwell and his penny nails. At a track meet, Chuck was scheduled to throw the javelin, and he hoped to break the state record. He had flirted with it at several previous meets, he was well rested, and he was performing in a good wind before the home crowd.

But something went terribly wrong. He miscalculated on the crucial throw and hurled the javelin like a spear, right through Coach's neck.

Coach had been bearing down without mercy on the geeks, the gamers, the gearheads, and the ones like me who kept our heads inside a book. All of us had been designated to carry water for the jocks. During the track meet Maxwell had made his way onto the field to pound fourpenny nails wherever he could. Coach had caught him red-handed. When Chuck made his fateful toss, Coach was swinging his paddle wildly above Maxwell's skull, so the javelin took him completely by surprise. Flailing his arms wildly, he went down, pinned like a biology specimen to the grassy infield, the paddle still flapping spasmodically. He had taught Chuck everything he knew about the javelin, had directed him through his every stage performance, and at one pep rally had claimed to love him like a son.

After a few paralyzed moments, Chuck, his arm still dangling before him, tried to rush to Coach. Everyone could see what he wanted to do: yank away the javelin and make things right, reverse time, change the fabric of reality. And probably he would have done it—that's how magical his charisma was—but his teammates restrained him.

Two medical technicians rushed to the stricken coach. As delicately as Boy Scouts they unfastened him, like unpegging the corner of a tent, and gently placed him on a stretcher, the javelin still in his neck. They had to cut it with a hacksaw before they could maneuver him into the waiting ambulance. Miraculously, Coach was alert the entire time, able to wave his paddle to the shocked spectators before the ambulance, its siren bleeping, rushed him to surgery.

30

Maxwell nodded knowingly, his lips pursed in triumph, and pointed to his nearby book bag, which was clunky with his silver hammer and what was left of a pound of fourpenny nails.

Though I was shocked by the accident, I had to stifle a laugh when Coach went down like one of the fainting girls. I didn't know what to do with my mixed emotions. I imagined the javelin holding my father to the ground during one of his drinking bouts when he swung his belt instead of a paddle at any part of my body he could reach.

Coach was finally taken off the critical list and Chuck became himself again, as though he had walked into and out of somebody else's nightmare. Miraculously, Coach had only a nasty scar and that voice, high and sweet like Molly's, to remind us of his brush with death, and Chuck received a great outpouring of sympathy. "He's more human now, don't you think?" I overheard Molly say. "Now I can see he needs love and compassion more than the rest of us."

When I heard that, I wanted the son of a bitch dead like a doornail. I went looking for Maxwell, determined to ask him to conjure up more magic.

Even so, the day after *A Streetcar Named Desire*, I stood as ordered behind and slightly to Molly's side as Chuck and his phalanx approached. He was still strutting like Stanley, still the spit and image of Brando in the movie all of us had been forced to watch in English class, and I knew my work was cut out for me. We had also read *Julius Caesar* in English, and looking at Chuck it was easy to imagine Caesar in Rome, desperate petitioners reaching out with their pleas. Crossing up Chuck on his exalted plane was as unthinkable as betraying Caesar. Like Chuck, Caesar no doubt consoled a few with a clap on the back, an intimate nod. He probably nudged others in a generous show of affection, deigning to treat a second-string senator as his peer. For the girls, Chuck had his patented vague smile, that sensuously full underlip slightly curled at the corners. His smile, sometimes aided by a hooded wink, was usually what did them in. First a sigh, then a rolling of the eyes, and finally a seasick swaying before the swoon. Chuck took them down like deadfall.

That day, when he seemed most like a deity, I revived Molly with the medical device from the philanthropist: a vial of smelling salts so strong it would make a dead horse kick. "Never rely on the kindness of a stranger," I murmured, waving the salts like a wand before her upturned, neighing nostrils, cradling her gently and smelling her soapy aroma. "Take advantage of the one who loves you."

Her eyes fluttered and her mouth opened in a bright smile. She laughed. "Gotcha," she said. "I don't faint, even over a dreamboat like him." For a moment we were intimate and carefree, as if lying alone on a checkered blanket in a prairie field full of high grass with a picnic basket beside us. It was a moment of camaraderie, of joyous freedom, that I've seldom managed to find again. It was as if Chuck had magically transferred some of his charisma to me. Then she stared away to the cafeteria. "Did you see him in *Streetcar?*" she asked.

I stood and pulled her to her feet. I stared darkly at her. I didn't say a word.

"Wasn't it the loveliest thing you ever saw? He was *wonderful*, like one of those statues come to life. We get to live in the Time of Chuck. Are we lucky to have him here among us, or what?" She laughed again, this time so hard she had trouble catching her breath.

"Got me for the second time," I said.

It was her valedictory. Before I could stammer out a reply, one of her girlfriends touched her on a wrist and she was gone, and so was Chuck.

A year later, I happened upon her wedding announcement in the local paper one Sunday. My mother had died and I lived alone. I worked in the oil fields as a roughneck, a job that didn't suit me at all, and saved most of my pay so I could get to college. It was spring and flowers were brightly in blossom after a hard winter. Molly wore a wedding dress and looked about the same in the black-and-white snapshot as she had when she jogged in her khaki outfit to the gym, always running late and then stopping at the door to leap high like Chuck when he slam-dunked a basketball.

As my own valedictory, I drove to the high school on a day of deep clouds and found my way to the wooden bench where I had spent so much time for four years. It was summer. The campus was hot and deserted, the grass gone brown.

I ran my rough hands over the bench's rotting wooden slats. I could see the bright glare of the water tower. Chuck was long gone, of course, playing football at the state university in Fargo—still a success but no longer making anybody faint—and I remembered that he had once declared the Rosetta Stone to be a ski slope in the Rocky Mountains.

Oddly enough, those memories, unlike Chuck's fame or my crush on Molly, haven't faded with time. And I've come to understand that my life's vocation, one sentence following another, is to climb into the clouds as if they are mountains and rappel down their slopes, deciphering their whorls and hieroglyphics as if I hold between my fingers a key to some indecipherable understanding.

It gives me hope in dark times.

Ava's Demon

He comes home and beats me, like my father once did. "How many do you want?" He uses a thick leather belt, black like obsidian, one he keeps under the sink with the whiskey and the fix. He's like Hemingway: a quart a day.

"As many as you think." I find the will to submit. It's come to that. My voices have deserted me; my ears ring.

He smiles afterward, takes me to the mattress, does the nasty, fixes me good, puts me asleep, the sleep of the dead. He paints. In the morning when I wake, he covers the easel with cloth. After breakfast he leaves, canvas still covered. With his paints and brushes and sketchpad and a dark hooded jacket, he's gone all day. He returns at dusk, the wind sweeping the shore, the canvas shrouded.

"Why can't I see? Wasn't that the vow we made?"

"Keep off my back." Mud's caked on his shoes. "You're always on my back." He takes off his shoes. As I buff the leather, losing myself in the creases, odd creatures hover around me and he paces, comes close, leans over and grunts, then stalks to the wood-burning stove. He stares into the grate. "You're getting lost," he says. "There's only the strap. Nothing else can do."

* * *

"My name's Pablo," he said the first time we met. "Painting's my game. Want to see my etchings?"

"Do you really have etchings?" He was a rugged man with grayish crusty hair, blue eyes that strayed to my cleavage, dark, radioactive skin that glowed.

"They're very good," he said, taking a slug from his flask. He moved close. I could see corrugations of thought under the brim of his sailor's cap, tilted at a rakish angle. "Everyone says so."

"Everyone?"

He grinned. "My former wives, at least. You can't get more critical than that."

His rage started in one of the wars. On the boat his comrades celebrated respite. "The waves," he shouted. "The way they move. Make them stop!" He ran the upper deck, whipping his mates with his belt, sailor's knife lashed to his leg. He broke a jaw, ruptured a spleen. They cracked him upside the skull, left a forehead indentation, put him in restraints, gagged him, tossed him in the brig. "Let me out!" he screamed. "I did it for your good; it's not over. None of it's over. Let me out!" They let him scream. Exhausted, he made promises. "Adrenal exhaustion," he told me. "My whole endocrine system got fucked up. My lizard brain took over." They threatened court-martial, discharged him. "Back-in-the-world deserves you," they said. He grew a beard, lived in a garret in Fargo, of all places, alternated between orgies and solitude. "Like a priest," he said. "I

36

lived in the place where Bob Dylan once lived, though at the time he called himself Elston Gunn."

One night he screamed out such bile that neighbors called the cops. When they arrived, he pulled off his belt. "Back off," he said. "I'm no man to tangle."

* * *

On the island in the Boundary Waters, I cook eggs. He likes them over easy. "Isn't this better than that city hustle, all that crap? Aren't we better here?" He likes his coffee hot, oily, black.

I stare across the water at the skyline of the broken city, an illusion made by clouds and landscape and the shit in my veins. It's where I come to myself. Abuse on the farm before Mama left with me for good, but I'd been ruined by then—rude, graceless, high on anything, child-waitress and sometimes prossie at the café, where I learned everything I need to know about men. Back with Mama, running from my brutal father. "You don't yet have wings," she said, "and yet already want to fly." She did what she could. It didn't help. I couldn't make it through. The only thing that made any sense was Poe: "Over the mountains of the moon/ Down the valley of the shadow/ Ride, boldly ride, the shade replied/ If you seek for Eldorado." I had a child, poor thing. Named Serena, the most beautiful name in the world. She's with Mama, who I hope does better by her than I did. It breaks me to think of her.

I tried, though, I like to think; I did try.

He gulps coffee like a drunk, cup after cup. "Listen. You're mine; I'm yours. Repeat it." He walks to the sink, pausing twice to stare at my legs, then bends over, rises, stretches, shakes his head. "Sometimes my hands do more."

"What am I learning?" My head turns gauzy; voices haunt me like the hazy landscape. "What's the point?"

"Pleasure," he says. "Nothing's like anything." He pauses when the horn bleeps across the island. "Listen. You hear? The monster!"

The words are so stupid, I laugh. He glares, thinks twice, and laughs too.

His eyes wide like pennies, he reaches for a pair of shades. "Put on your dark glasses. This could be the end. Let's go stand on the beach and watch for the cloud. You hear that siren?"

* * *

"Your etchings, they don't make sense," I said that first night.

He raised his chin and looked away, face dark like raw meat. "Not everyone knows how to see what's there." His face, sunburned, frowned its network of lines. On his forehead a large vein pulsed. He moved close, the force of his presence beating me dizzy. "What, you think I'm new? I've had four wives. *Four*—and they all loved me. That was way back in the day."

He dreamed me into his life. He pulled a magic marker from his camouflage jacket and scrawled a wide scar across an etching. "All my paintings have predicted tonight," he said and led me to the sofa, where he fixed me and did me. A week later I moved in, safe, hidden from all the eyes. He was going to be my Poe, my voice, the voice in our heads. "I'll take you to the Boundary Waters. You can be my muse. I've got acres. No electricity, no phone," he said, sailor's cap awry, a dog-killing grin on his face. "Electricity supports the monsters. We'll live like Robert and Elizabeth Browning, like John and Yoko, Kurt and Courtney, Stieglitz and O'Keeffe." I laughed and he grinned. "Just the two of us, by candlelight. We'll have one another, in the custody of the cosmos."

38

* * *

On Saturday, when he lets me leave the camp, we picnic. I bring chicken, deviled eggs, bread. He takes me where the waves lap ashore. We walk sandy pockets of trees colored like cinnamon; far away, on private land, a beach umbrella stretches people out, stick figures. They get up, spasticate to the shore, and lie at the water's edge.

"It's a robot convention," I say.

He laughs so hard he can't get back his breath. "What do you think you see?" he says. "There's nobody out there. It's just the Boundary Waters."

He gives me my fix. "You know I stabbed one of my wives? With a Bic pen," he adds. "She didn't even need surgery." He turns and opens his mouth several times like a fish, as though clearing his ears of static. "But that was then. This is now."

My blood courses like plastic melt in a rubber hose. Patty melt, that's what we used to call them at the café. Cheese like liquid, burger burned to a crisp, toast. He coos, pulls me into scrub oak and sand, does me good and nasty. Afterward, civil, he slings an arm around me. "To hell with the sexual slave. I want the child. Where's the child?"

In stop-and-step gestures, I climb out of my dress and dance us home, twirling in leprechaun fashion. I can't dance. I'm a klutz, fixed or stone cold sober, but it doesn't matter to him or to me.

"Get the rattle." He bites his lip, drawing blood. "God, that's beautiful. Now shake it. Shake it."

"How long?"

"Don't question the cosmos!" He roughs me up a little. "Feel how things are." I start coughing, can't stop. "That's what counts." He cracks his neck. Shadows play on his face, alive in the light of the lantern. His eyes settle on the world inside his head. "Be who you are." He stands with his canvas. "Outside, though. I need myself."

No electricity, no running water; only the stove, the well, some kerosene, the lantern's shifting light. A big steak knife. His canvas is life: He paces, glowers in the light, cracks his knuckles. Agitated, the lines of his face on fire, he crunches to my side. "What have you done? Can't you see the stars, how they break? Tell me what you've done to the waves! Can't you see?" He heaves a stone into the water. "How many?" he asks, rage twisting his face.

I cringe, wrapped in a sheet, in his crazy vision, and bow my head. It's the way things are. His hands move in delicate brushlike gestures and he stumbles to the canvas. "Let me be. Can't you ever let me be?"

Outside on a damp rock I notice the moon change the tide into a new world. The eyes of animals thick under the sea. I smooth wrinkles in the rocks, but they vanish, slippery-green. The water clings to my sheet like the green inside his whiskey. The moon stitches together stars with light as I stroke the rocks asleep.

* * *

Wind, scissors, paper. One breaks, one cuts, one covers.

"What do you want?" the wind asks.

"Let me be! Let me be! Let me be!"

One sound—the one a sentence makes, the one that belongs to me—rises and falls with the life of his paint.

In the day he takes nothing, doesn't return until dusk, but the timbre of his voice fills the camp. He's everywhere—on the mattress, in the food, under the sink, in the cracks between the planks. His cape gestures about me. "You see yourself in everyone's face. They still live inside you. Your goddamn mama. Your goddamn Serena." He takes out the strap. "It's the genes, bitch," he says. "It's all in the genes. Let's clean out those genes."

"Fix me," I shout; "fix me good!"

40

* * *

The motor launch snuggles into the dock with his buddies, who bring food, alcohol, drugs, a woman. He puts me in the closet.

"Why? Can't I see other faces?"

"No. You've got to get away from eyes."

In the closet, roaches and mice have eyes that glow in the dark. Voices from another planet tell him the city: the shouts, the jokes, the firefights, the wars, the creeping pestilence taking so many lives, the Marauders in which they all take pleasure. "Where's the *puta*?" he calls out. "Where's the *puta*? Don't tell me, let me see! Give me the *puta*!" He doesn't mean me. They bring in the woman. He unstacks canvases for her. "Wow," she says. "You're an ace. How do you do that stuff? Where does it come from?"

"It's all where you focus your eyes."

"Your eyes are as bad as the rest," I mumble in the closet. He's no better, no worse. It's their eyes he wants to keep me from—the others, the old ones, stored in the dusty crates, stretched thin. Tokens of my life, maps of moments. *Every creator breeds dissent*, my voices tell me. *Avatars approach our graves. Only drifters escape respite: He's a drifter! Not an exile, not an artist! A drifter! From that log, that splinter!* I listen, take it all in, turn cryptic advice into code, and when he opens the closet, I stay. *There is more time than life*, the voices say. He cajoles, subdued, apologetic, senses something has changed. He walks the room, sprawls on the bed.

"Let me be," he mutters in his sleep and wakes a day late, smiling, brow drawn. "Be the child. I want the child." He puts the bonnet in my hands. *Don't take it out your soul.* I drop the bonnet. "Be the child; let me have the child!" He looks at the sink. "Don't you want your fix?"

"No. Too much you, not enough me." My hand brushes the table.

"Bury your voices. *I'm* the cosmos." He slaps me. "You feel? You feel how things are?"

I walk to the shrouded canvas. "You don't spend your days with paint."

"Don't you want your fix, sweetheart?" He's playful, dogface low-down sly. "You shaky?" He turns to the stove, hands clenched, face like a piece of meat. "I'll take it straight out your flesh." He bends over. Now or never. I imagine my entire weight putting the steak knife where his heart should be, listen for the sound it makes when I crank it, like gristle trying to speak.

"The monster!" Fixed good, strap in hand, veins a-bulge, breathing hard, eyes a puzzle, he falls at my feet into his own blood and hacks across the floor, one hand caressing the vision before him. "Let me be. You let me be."

His eyes disappear.

Figures in robes spattered with paint climb into boxes of wood.

"How many do you want?" they shout.

I wake to the moon, an addict longing for a fix. I think of my child, Serena. I say her name. Once. Twice. A thousand times. Time passes. Hours, days, weeks? It's time to make my way back to where she might be. In the patterns and cycles of sleep, with wind and water an echo, all the voices, for the rest of my life, are like the sound of a sentence, emerging only to fade.

Election Day

"Did you vote?" the mysterious Ava said. She had a bright orange sticker stuck to the sweater over her left nipple. "I VOTED," it said. She had come to the barbecue with our neighbor Bobbi, whether as a long-lost friend returned from the Boundary Waters—where Bobbi intimated some terrible things had occurred—or as a newfound lover, I had no idea.

Time would tell. It always does.

"Vote? There's an election today?" I was having her on, of course. I knew there was an election. Everybody told me it was important, that it would change everything if the wrong creep got into office.

"You registered?" she said. I was dumbfounded. How could any responsible citizen decide not to vote or pretend not to understand what was at stake? Did she ever stop to think that my vote might neutralize hers?

Or was she having me on? There was a furious light in her blue eyes. She glowed as if on fire with rail-thin luminosity. She had survived a long recovery after the Boundary Waters, Bobbi had warned, and could be brittle. That much Bobbi had told us as prelude to our gathering. "I'm bringing her along with trepidation. Give her slack. It's her first outing in a while."

"Of course I'm registered," I said. "What do you take me for?"

I voted. I could tell you who for. It's still a free country, despite the mess, the violence, the new world order. The ballot is still secret. I'm secret too. You can't know about me.

We stood on the porch that faced my next-door neighbor Park's large bur oak, a majestic tree that could outlive not only election day but all of us who presently walk the Earth. Ava was very easy on my eyes, but her own ocean blue ones stared deep at everything around her, as if she thought she had X-ray vision. I nursed a gin and tonic and thought about politics. There was a lot to think about: things to curse, things to praise, people who should be shot, a few worth celebrating. I could have ranted and raved, and I knew that eventually I would, but I decided I would hold off as long as possible.

I thought I would wend my way inside later in the evening, after our guests were gone, and turn on the television to study the election results and curse if needed, shout with delight if things turned out good. My friend Denzel and his wife, Latesha, drove into the driveway on the other side of the house and my wife, Louise, greeted them with a happy shriek. I grimaced. I wanted to say something to her about that shriek, which had become more frequent of late, but she would be offended. Everything offended her if it wasn't straight-out praise. So I kept quiet and kept the peace. Louise had lived a hard life before we found each other. If she enjoyed a shriek now and then, so be it. There was little enough joy left in our part of the world.

After a few minutes of conversation that I could hear inside the house, Denzel came out juggling his own gin and tonic, a fresh one

44

for me, and a glass of Chardonnay for the mysterious Ava. His hold on the drinks was precarious, as if he might drop one. He had a little too much weight around the middle, a recent development, though who am I to talk? He gave Ava her drink and introduced himself. Before she could hypnotize him or bore into him with those eyes, I stood, put my drink on a table next to the grill, and shook his hand with a tight, firm grip so that he would know my spirits were up. "Did you vote?" I asked.

"Hell, yeah," he said, smirking, used to my antics. I could tell you who he voted for in my sleep. The world has gone to hell in a bushel basket. The weather won't behave itself. The people up here in this part of the world are dying off or driving off. There's unrest. Violence. Marauders out west who, like the weather, might show up with a shit show in mind. Some nights, we have armored vehicles parked on the periphery of the neighborhood, special Militias paid for by the homeowner's association. Despite that, Denzel still doesn't carry a gun, which is ungodly behavior. What if a Marauder came along and grabbed Latesha by the ass and threw her to the ground? What's he going to do about it without a concealed carry? Somebody I don't like puts their paws on Louise? *Boom!*

We didn't talk politics, though. We talked sports. We talked food. We talked books. We both like mysteries, the kind they write in Scandinavia, where life is kind of good and all the people are treated mostly the same while mass murderers ply their trade, but only in fiction, until a woman with a dragon tattoo or a man with a deep scar across his face snaps them in two.

Ava ignored our chatter and stared, twiddling her long-stemmed glass, at the awesome oak. In profile she was a stunner—Ava, I mean, with the long neck of an Egyptian queen, an aristocratic Roman nose, and décolletage that could slay a man. Her skin was dark, glistening, and I wondered where she came from, where her parents might have been born. Dark skin, blue eyes. The colored tattoos on her upper

45

arms were unreadable hieroglyphs, abstract patterns that reminded me of paint Jackson Pollock might drip on canvas. Her jeans were tight, her sleeveless blouse bright and Latin. There was something otherworldly about her, as if she had arrived in a time machine and might vanish without warning.

Louise was inside with Latesha and Bobbi, all of them making a Tater Tots hot dish and a strawberry-rhubarb pie to accompany the grass-fed beef and very wild salmon I planned to put on the grill. Maybe Bobbi would reveal some Ava scuttlebutt to Louise and Latesha, and Louise might clue me in later, if the women didn't keep what they learned to themselves. It was clear to me that Ava would be the prime topic of conversation if she wasn't with us. "What's the story with Ava?" one of us would say, probably me, though it would be Louise who would tease out of Bobbi whatever she knew.

They were making pie, but I was the real cook that night: steak medium rare on the grill. It's a steak that's very lean. Lots of protein. Easy to overcook. A little charring never hurts a good steak, but these babies are delicate. I got them special at Mike's Meats. Mike knows meat, and I know Mike. The salmon is for Bobbi, who's pescatarian.

Ava told me she eats anything. "Not particular. Food is food."

"Did I tell you I voted?" I said when the conversation died down. "Did my duty?" Denzel agreed that it might be good later to watch the results, but the weather was too grand on the deck to go inside, and nobody wanted to be the first to stare into a phone. The clouds were deep and fluffy. If I didn't know better, I'd think they were mountains. The usual haze from the city twenty miles down the interstate had been blown in our direction earlier in the day. City stink. But the wind stayed high, and the stink moved on.

I heard the kind of beep a truck makes when it backs up. "FRED'S TREES," the logo read. There was a picture of a logger with a saw taking down a big one. Park, my neighbor, came out to greet the tree man. That would be Fred, I guessed, though it's possible Fred's Trees

46

was not a one-man operation. It was possible that Fred didn't work alone. In fact, there was another man in the truck with him.

The two of them talked for a few minutes. Fred was a very tall Black man who wore a bright orange uniform and angled his right hand with his white work glove to indicate to Park something about the tree. I got a funny feeling. If what I thought was about to happen came to pass, I realized that I would have a situation on my hands. I picked up the fresh gin and tonic and drank it. Fast.

"What do you think they're doing over there?" I asked.

"Looks like a tree's coming down," Denzel said. "Is there more blight in the area?"

"Not that I know of," I said.

Ava had turned to listen, licking her lips and sipping her wine. "They kill trees, don't they?" she said in a droll voice.

"Huh." Denzel frowned. He didn't know what to say to that. He wasn't a tree hugger, that's for sure, but nature was one of his issues, with the seas rising, the heat burning the land, the crazy storms dropping like napalm without warning. "I hope they're not taking down that big oak just to improve the view."

He read my mind. That was my thought exactly. "Let's not jump to conclusions," I said. "There are other trees on his property. Or maybe they're talking about a trim, some pruning." I heard myself say the words, but I was getting a bad feeling, a vibe, and could feel anger build to a crescendo.

"He's a man on his own land, right?" Ava said. She tucked a stray hair behind her ears, squeezed her lower lip with two fingers. One of her nails was bitten to the quick. "You men do what you like on your land, all of you; isn't that the way it is?"

I ignored her. "You know what, Denzel? I think Park is going to take down that tree."

By now we were both frowning and studying the situation as if we were watching a postapocalyptic movie. "Fred, if that's Fred," I said, "is there to erase a beautiful bur oak from Park's backyard."

"Dude, it's his yard," Ava said. "His tree. It's a great tree, no doubt he should leave it unless it's diseased. But that's not for you to decide. None of your business."

"Hell with that," I said, though I tried to soften my tone to placate the mysterious Ava. "How many oaks like that are left in the world?"

"Plenty," she said. "You'd be surprised."

"Is that a bigot speaking?" I said.

She startled as if struck. "Dude," she said, "stick it up your ass. Who the fuck do you think you are?"

She went on like that. She had a bee in her bonnet. I ignored the rant, though Denzel was scowling, maybe in shock. "I thought you were a nature boy," I said to him. "Tree hugger stuff. That tree has a right to its own existence. Just like Ava here. Let's you and me go over there and see if we can't save it."

He demurred. "She's right. His yard."

What I figured. Didn't have the courage of his convictions. "He's gonna rape that tree right in front of us, and this is your response?" I was disgusted.

"Rape?" Ava said. "Not the right word, dude. Reconsider your vocabulary."

I could hear the ladies in the kitchen giggle. Sound carries. White wine. That's what they were drinking. White wine makes for the giggles. Ava heard the laughter, noticed her Chardonnay was gone, stared me a dagger for good measure, and left us to join the ladies. She looked a bit sketchy on her feet, but that stare could kill.

I sighed and walked across the yard, which was freshly mowed and smelled sweet like wildflowers and clipped grass, a smell so unique that I would remember it if I was on Mars. Our house didn't have trees out back or in front. They had all died from the latest blight.

We all lived in a suburb on the western edge of town. Beyond it was farmland green with young crops. Most of the trees out there were young, unlike the bur oak, which was majestic, the kind of tree that kids can climb, a tree to conjure with. It's the kind of tree that neighbors should worship and spend money to save. My guess is that Park would have sent the tree to an assisted-living facility, the way his fussy wife did with her mother when the old woman's memory went, but you can't uproot and transplant an old oak the way you can a senile old woman.

"Hey!" I shouted. "Park!"

He turned from Fred, if the tree man's name was Fred. Fred had a clipboard in one hand and a pencil in the other. He was so tall that I wondered if he had played basketball in his gone days. What I realized as I put it all together while closing the rest of the distance between us is that they were talking about logistics. Old Park didn't want the tree falling on his house after it was cut. "Gerald?" he asked.

I put a friendly hand on his shoulder. He's a small man. Asian. I tower over him like a medieval knight in armor come a calling, though Fred's height puts me to shame. "I couldn't help but notice, Park," I said, as friendly as a man selling insurance. "You seem to be contemplating doing something to this magnificent bur oak that all your neighbors love to death."

Park shrugged my hand away and moved a few steps to one side so that Fred stood between him and me. "This gentleman is here to cut it down today. His name is Fred. Have you met him?" I could tell that he was determined to be polite.

I nodded at Fred up there above me. "That's not going to happen," I said. I pointed to the tree. "That lady is no tramp." I heard somebody call my name and turned to stare at my deck. My wife, Louise, stood there with a spatula in one hand and Denzel by her side with his arms crossed. She waved the spatula as if it was a wand. *Get your fat ass back here* is what she was saying. *Fire up the grill.*

49

Bobbi and Ava, glasses of Chardonnay in hand, clinked them together. Louise pointed to the grill and squatted next to it to turn on the propane. Latesha was lying in a lounge chair with her head rolled back to take in the last of the day's sun, which had come out from hiding.

Ava walked toward me. Was she an emissary from Louise?

"Your wife has the right idea," Park said. "I'm within my rights. The tree has to go. It occludes my view, and its roots could damage my foundation." He was polite. There was no combativeness in his voice. "I agree it's a nice tree. If we could dig it up and let you have it, we would do so. Can't be done."

"Park, have you ever read Pliny?" I said.

He frowned. "Pliny? I think I've heard the name. But no. The answer is no."

"You haven't read him?"

"That's right."

"Let me share with you something Pliny once wrote. They called him Pliny the Elder. Wisdom in that last word. This is what he said: 'An object in possession seldom retains the same charm as it had in pursuit.'"

Park blinked, trying to puzzle it out. Fred with his clipboard watched us argue the way a coach at a game studies the cat-and-mouse combat on the court. He looked at his watch. Park noticed.

"This is all very amusing," he said, "but this man here is on a schedule to keep." He motioned for the clipboard and pencil and scrawled a signature on the paper. "That gives him permission to work. One of his associates is sitting in the truck and will help with the job."

"You don't understand," I said. "That tree's not coming down. It belongs to all of us. Not just to you. I love that tree. I've lived with it for years, since before you bought this house. This tree is not yours to cut down."

Ava came up beside Park. "Dudes," she said. "Dudes. Can we talk this out? Can we just get along?" I could hear that she was imitating

50

somebody. She squeezed the narrow bridge of her nose. "A tree like this should be treasured." She was a little drunk. Or a lot drunk.

"Hello," Park said politely. "Your host is making a fuss about something that's none of his business. If he doesn't back off, I'm going to call the constabulary."

"Possession is nine-tenths of the law, Park? That what you're saying?"

"No, Gerald. I'm saying possession is all of the law. Everything."

"The constabulary?" Ava said, tasting the quaint word. She closed in on Park and whispered something to him that I couldn't hear. He squinted. This was none of her business, he was thinking. Fred up there in the clouds didn't look none too happy about the delay. A glance passed like radar between him and Park.

"Did you vote, Park?" I said.

That stopped him. "None of your business, Gerald."

Fred had his signature. That was enough for him. He and his co-worker carried a ladder to the tree. They had ropes, pulleys, other paraphernalia required in the tree-cutting business. We all took a brief break from our conversation to watch them install the pulley and rope with an anchor hammered into the ground so that the tree, when it fell, would fall away from the house. "Park," I said again. "You voted? You didn't say."

Ava shivered. She looked sketchy again, hugging herself and squeezing, as if her blood wasn't pumping through her body right. "Dudes? This is macho bullshit." She turned again to Park. "Park? If I may? Why not take a night to think it over?"

"Not a bad idea," I said. It was indeed a smart thing for her to say, but I could tell she was edgy with the standoff. I thought she might be about to blow. I thought it might be interesting if I saw what that looked like.

Whatever it was, her sensible words or her impatient tone, it hit Park the wrong way. He set his mouth in a scowl. "What if you were big with child," he said to Ava, ignoring me, "and didn't want the baby? What if a man who didn't own your body made you learn that he could tell you what to do, make you keep the baby? Would you like that, lady?"

I could see her face turn pale, as if the blood was being siphoned from it. A bad memory, I thought. In fact, a law that would do exactly that was on the ballot. "Oh, dude," she said. "This is your house. Your land. I get that. You can murder that fucking tree for all I care. You can do whatever the fuck you want. Fuck a duck while you're at it." She twerked her pelvis as if fucking. "I get that too. Way of the world and all that shit. Then you can see it die all over again at night in your dreams. You know how awful that is? To watch something you've killed die, over and over again, every goddamned night?"

"Lady, I say again. You would do to me and my land what men do to women and their bodies." He walked away and pulled out his phone. The local constabulary. As if they don't have enough to keep them occupied in these times. I knew some of the local cops. Which one would come? If it was Peter—Peter Pumpkin Eater, I called him to his face—there might be trouble. There had been some trouble with Peter in the past. He and I had once come to blows. I couldn't remember over what. Nothing, actually. Nothing at all.

I walked over to Park. Once he shut down the phone, I told him that voting was a sacred rite of passage for real Americans. "What you mean by that?" Park said.

"Take it how you want." I stepped close, inside his personal space. "No damage done yet to that magnificent oak. Why not stop?" Fred climbed the ladder to lop off some of the tree's branches. The point of no return was fast approaching.

Ava spoke to me. "Dude, he's right." She finished her wine like water, stared at her glass as if she couldn't believe it was empty, and tossed it at Park's feet like a bouquet of flowers. She stared down at it. "I can't believe I did that," she said. "Macho bullshit."

"Macho?" I said. "This tree is a wise woman. Nothing macho about that."

"How does your wife put up with your crap?" Ava said. "Bobbi tells me she might be leaving you soon." She smirked when she saw me taken aback. I knew it was a lie.

As if on cue, Bobbie and Louise, like cyborgs on batteries, hailed us from my deck. Louise flipped her head to get a loop of hair out of her line of sight, motioned with her glass of wine, calling me back from the brink. Many nights, she and I, pickled with booze, argued for hours about anything that came to mind. "Big Ger," she would say, "you're mentally ill." It was our kind of fun. She had the right to call me out. The mysterious Ava didn't.

Ava pulled her hair back behind her head into a ponytail. She looked dazed.

"This isn't your fight," I said. "Why don't you go wait with Denzel and the ladies?"

But Denzel had approached without me seeing him and now stood beside me. "Dude," he said, mocking Ava, "it's his damn yard. It's his tree. Let it be."

Ava hummed a song under her breath, a ditty I could almost remember from the gone days. The gin in my brain was making me hear an echo, a refrain, as if the earth itself vibrated beneath my feet. I swear to God, I'm not a violent man, not by any means, but I wanted to punch her goddamn lights out. Denzel too. "Get thee all to a nunnery," I said, mocking them both. "Either you're in this fight to the end or you're not."

"Not," Ava said.

Denzel shrugged. "I wash my hands of it, Gerald. Also, we're all getting hungry."

"Hey, Park," I called, as if the Asian were half a block away, "you didn't tell me if you voted. Did you vote? And how did you vote? As a feminist, I want to know if you believe a woman has the right to choose."

Ava turned to Denzel. "This asshole? He's your buddy?"

"None of your business," Park said. "This is still the United States, Gerald."

"Are you sure about that?" I said. "Have you been paying attention lately?"

Ava walked back to the deck very slowly, as if she didn't know the way or was terrified she might trip on a blade of grass. I watched her take her time.

Denzel crowded me. "Let's go cook some food," he said. My blood rose and I nudged him hard. I remembered how a friend, after two years in the military, told me that overseas under fire he could keep his cool most of the time, but now and then he saw red mist instead of air and went batshit crazy. "Hey, Park," I shouted. "When the cops arrive, I'm going to ask them to take a look at your papers. Are you legal, my friend?"

The blood drained from Denzel's face. "A bridge too far," he said. He retreated and followed the mysterious Ava across the green lawn to the deck. They all sat there on deck chairs as if on the *Titanic*. Louise opened two more bottles of wine. I expected that she was unhappy with me. The wine would help with that.

Park crossed his arms, checked his watch. For the next ten minutes, until the constabulary arrived, I lectured him on nature, ecology, and the secret life of trees. I told him about the root system that was crying out in pain. I told him the tree was sending out a banshee wail to every other tree. "That tree is a magnificent woman," I said. "Imagine if I cut your wife's throat with a slice-and-dice knife. That tree is about to feel the way you would feel if I did that."

"Is that something you might do, Gerald?" Park said, his vocal fry revealing his stress.

"Imagine it," I said. "Imagine how that would feel."

The cop car arrived and pulled into a vacant spot next to Fred's tree truck. Fred, seeing the cavalry, started up his chain saw, moved

54

to the oak, and made a cut into the trunk away from the house at an angle from above. It was a deep gash, maybe a quarter of the way into the gnarled trunk, just below a burl that might be saved and polished and made into an ashtray.

I walked over to Fred and reached out to grab him at the elbow of the hand holding the saw, but Peter—it was Peter in the cop car, burly Peter with his cross around his mottled neck as if he was the disciple and not a local rube with his belly jingling like a cow's udder—wrenched me from behind, threw me down, and fell on top of me like a sack of grain. He cuffed me. "What the fuck," I said, feeling my shoulder wrench, breathing in the smell of grass and soil, and turning my head to one side to catch my breath. "Get the hell off me, Pumpkin Eater."

Breathing hard, Peter pulled himself up, fiddled with his uniform some, and then helped me to my feet, wrenching me up with the help of the handcuffs, which caused searing pain. For the next twenty minutes, after I caught my breath, there was a heated discussion. "Listen," Peter finally said, "this tree is entirely in his yard. This community does not have a heritage tree ordnance. I looked it up. The trunk of this tree stands completely on Park's land. That means it belongs exclusively to him."

"The root system," I said. "You're forgetting the roots."

Peter stared me down and continued. "If you had wanted to protect this tree, you could have brought it up to the homeowner's association. You didn't. Now, sir, it's too late. Mr. Park has the right to do what he's doing." He caught his breath. He was winded. "Besides, don't you folks—don't all of us?—have more important things to worry about these days?"

"It's murder, isn't it?" I said. "You're condoning murder, aren't you?"

Peter shrugged and raised his eyes to heaven. He conferred with Park. He blew out a deep breath and perp-walked me not to his car but to my deck, where a G&T, the ice cubes melted, still sat on the round table beside my sun chair. I turned in time to see Fred make another gash, this one horizontal, in the bur oak deep enough to meet the first cut, which really is the deepest, I thought, and made a notch so that the oak would fall like a shot.

Ava was far away, in another country, the Boundary Waters maybe, her eyes bright, polychromatic. "You're lit up, aren't you?" I said. "Wish I was too." She didn't hear me, but the others wouldn't look my way. Even so, they made my case with due diligence to Peter that seeing a resplendent oak cut down in the prime of its long life drove a stake through my heart that had to bleed when it was pulled out. "Damn right," I muttered, though now, embarrassed myself, my voice sounded feeble. I had nothing more to say. Louise smiled as if one of our knock-down arguments had gone in her favor. "Gerry means well," she said. She smiled sweetly, but I could tell she wanted to say something mean. And would, later, when we were alone.

"This settled, then?" Peter said. "Park won't have to call me back?" We all agreed. Peter uncuffed me. "Sorry about that, sir," he said. He held out his hand.

"Hell," I said. I took it.

He shambled across the lawn to Park. They talked as if discussing the result of a blind date, whether any sparks had been struck, and then Peter turned to Fred and gave him a thumbs-up.

Peter and Park continued their talk. Both nodded twice. They shook hands once. Peter came back to us, and I laughed at his Santa Claus belly. "Santa Claus," I said with bitterness, "about to give me a gift." That's what he did. "Mr. Park has agreed not to press charges," he said. He had a high-pitched voice that sounded like the squeal of a mouse and made me laugh. It wasn't a mean laugh. Such a big, clumsy man, such a tiny voice. "You know, I could charge you anyway if I feel like it. Public nuisance. Harassment. I'm only being nice for the sake of the neighborhood. This is one of the few that's still intact."

56

"Keep the peace and all that?" I said. Louise, sitting next to me in her own chair, pinched me hard. I felt emasculated and remembered what Ava had said about my wife's plans. Surely it was BS. "There's nothing to charge me with, and Park knows it."

Peter shrugged again; it was his conflict-resolution gesture. I could see Park stare my way with a smirk on his face and thought about charging across the lawn like a gorilla. But I'm not that—a gorilla, I mean—and so I held my place, stewing in my own juices, the steak still not grilled.

In the middle of this mental hullabaloo, the tree fell with an anti-climactic whoosh, hardly the earth-shaking atrocity I had imagined. But bad enough. The earth shook beneath my feet.

Bad enough.

I nodded and waved a hand like a wand. "Look over there." He did. I had to admire his equanimity. He could have put me in cuffs again just for the hell of it, to show me where things were at. My insides were boiling, but outside I was calm. My heart beat like a time machine taking me into a future I could only fear. I could see Peter pat himself on the back without moving a muscle. Another page from the new conflict-resolution package the local force received after a local young man in the right place at the wrong time was shot over nothing. "You see what I see?"

He pulled an ear as if turning on his battery and frowned. I nodded again. "Of course you do," I said. "You know what you see? Absence. There was presence there and now there's absence. Think of that when you wake at two in the morning to eat a doughnut. The something that was and the nothing that is."

"You know what I see, dude?" Ava said. "A line of trees on the horizon—oaks, maple, birch, even a healthy elm or two. Who gets to have those anymore? Appreciate what you got." She was talking about the faraway tree line a half mile beyond Park's place that separated our tract neighborhood from farmland.

"We've had reports of Marauders coming this way," Peter said. "If I were you, I'd make sure those armored vehicles are in place tonight."

There was a stump and a dead tree cut into pieces where the bur oak had been. It was private property and Park, whether he voted or not, could do with it what he wanted. Soon Fred would return with a stump grinder. In a day or a week there would be nothing but new grass seed where the majestic tree had stood its ground for so many years. Park could burn the wood from the oak in his fireplace.

Peter drove away in his constabulary car.

"Dude," Ava said, very relaxed after another long trip to the bathroom inside the house. "People tell me you're the man when it comes to steak. How about it? We're starving."

"Coming right up," I said. I've worked with junkies in the past. These days, who hasn't? I had no intention of starting anything. Even so, Bobbi stepped between us. Louise buried her face in her hands. Denzel folded his arms, turned, and stared into the middle distance. Latesha was half-dozing on the chaise longue. Ava grinned. "Whatever gets us through the days, right?"

I grilled the steak and salmon. We went inside and ate and drank and came back out, woozy with booze and protein, to sit and stare at the place where the tree had been. Louise brought out homemade rhubarb pie and a bottle of chilled dessert wine and five long-stemmed glasses, but the mood of the evening was dead. The five of them drank wine. I had a cognac. The mysterious Ava disappeared again into the house. When she returned, her skin almost glowed in the dark. Those blue eyes had a light in them that wouldn't go away. Whatever she stared at didn't have anything to do with us.

Past the dead tree, along the tree line where the houses stopped, armored vehicles groaned into their designated slots. The mercenaries we had hired eased out of the vehicles. One of them turned on some music—hard stuff, drums and shouts, some kind of call-and-response. We sipped our drinks and listened.

The oak in Park's yard was the first of many deaths in the neighborhood.

What's Good for the Goose Is Good for the Baba Ghanoush

This is the tale about what happened when Frankenstein (aka Frank-incense), the former talk show host, lately a volunteer on the border, where he worked with an endless stream of battered refugees, most of them kids, came out of retirement. Once an acclaimed broadcaster, his gray beard now a mess, he agreed to do a talk show, his forte, at the despoiled civic center in Fargo, North Dakota. It became what we now call the Week of Riots. He still had his signature low-pitched gravelly bass voice. His gray hair, once jet black, became so again, stained for the occasion, but he didn't touch what he called his baba ghanoush beard. His manner could still be smooth like flaxen grains of winter wheat when stimulated by an audience of any kind, the undercurrent of his laugh like the chop on a north Minnesota lake in a brisk wind. Or so we hoped.

His short, bald beauty of a buddy, Faust (aka Einstein) agreed to ride sidesaddle on stage, like in the old days, when talk show hosts had sidekicks, to provide wit and finesse if the script came apart, as it often did, making improvisation a must, but I grimaced at the thought. Faust had developed a tic as he aged that some compared to Tourette's syndrome, but Tourette's is an affliction, and Faust claimed that his incessant vulgarity was personal choice, a reaction to the times. Such language in Fargo, a town infantilized by church and state, could make for humiliation, disruption, chaos, and violence—maybe in that order, maybe not.

Even so, it was hope they sold. The two had lost a step from the stand-up glory days of long ago, when we compared them to Carson and Colbert, to Steve Allen and Richard Pryor, to Monty Python and the Marx Brothers, miscreants of a different order of insanity, but Frankenstein and Faust hadn't lost their comic timing. That was their pitch. Entertainers were great like that after the country lost its chutzpah and embraced its status as a banana republic, refusing to nationalize the banks or hold to account the crooks who decided the entire economy and all of its treasures belonged to the privileged few. Pandemics, autocratic leadership, minority rule, racial and ethnic strife, sexism, indentured servitude, and climate change disasters like you wouldn't believe. Women with minds of their own forced to have kids whether they wanted them or not. The troupers like Frankenstein and Faust did what they could to boost morale, working off the books for the good of us all, while the armed troopers and Militias, not to mention Marauders, busted heads and drank blood if that was the only nourishment at hand. Some in the Dakotas wore helmets with horns that made them look like the Vikings of old from the ancient Norwegian sagas. Ragnarok indeed: the Twilight of the Gods (also known as the despoilation of planet Earth).

In their glory days, they sometimes billed themselves as Franken-stein and Faust, sometimes as Frankincense and Einstein, depending

60

on the time of year. The big Christmas fete that featured an a cappella boy band of aging boomers was a crowd favorite. Because nostalgia. It brought out the Einstein in Faust and the Frankincense in Frankenstein. When they laughed, the crowd laughed with them. If they cried, which they seldom did, they would cry for us all, a great, weeping hullabaloo.

Only Frankenstein's personal friends knew his given name, and even most of them called him Frankie. When he wasn't on the border, he resided in an intentional community near Tulsa, what we once called a commune, where he found, he claimed, off-scale contentment milking goats, shearing sheep—his belly getting beach-ball big, as though pregnant—and sitting on a rocking chair in his happy place.

The truth, as I recall, was not like that. Everybody lied. It was the new truth.

Faust spent time there too, when he wasn't teaching local Fargo kids the new kinds of stuff they needed to know to survive in a failed state. Most Americans were no longer allowed to leave its borders. They carried too much disease. The rest of the world, except for the other failed states, was aghast at the recklessness, kinkiness, and complete irresponsibility of the millions of Americans whose prefrontal cortexes, the part of the brain that includes executive functions, including impulse control, had regressed. Many had the brains of irrepressible juvenile delinquents. They lived in a dystopia and called it exceptionalism. It was a national disease.

I call it Fantasyland. Heimlich, you might ask me, why? This story is the reason.

"They say go to Tulsa," Faust said, back in Fargo and happy to be home. "Tulsa. Know what, friend? I've been to Tulsa. It's a shithole."

That wasn't quite right. I too had joined that intentional community in hopes of finding peace and because, naively, I trusted Frankenstein and Faust not to lead me astray. There had been ninety of us living in the rugged foothills of eastern Oklahoma, what some call Green Country in those parts. All types, all kinds of creatures supposedly upholding the Ten Commandments but actually fornicating for the Lord, which they called the Eleventh Commandment. They named Frankenstein "Grandpa Frankincense," something to do with Christmas bounty and his leadership style. I was known as "Little Heimlich from North Dakota." I didn't mind it much. Didn't like it much, either. Faust often went by "Uncle Einstein" or "Brother Faust," depending whether he was being straight-out smart or just smartass. His own forte is telling shaggy dog stories that never stop. The "Never Ending Book," he calls it.

Sometimes I'd have to call out both of his names—"Faust! Einstein!"—to get his attention. "What say?" he'd answer. If he answered. "Who the fuck is that calling me way the fuck from Fargo? What are you doing here, Little Heimlich?"

I'm a nobody. He's a somebody. I don't mind.

When Frankenstein decided to leave the Oklahoma community for the southern border, an emergency mission of mercy in the company of his consort—a battle-ready woman with a good mind for business and handsome pecs strong enough to keep anybody in line—I took his place as in-house fixer for the commune. They told me to get stuff done while they fornicated and Bible-thumped, often with recording devices turned on.

Not much got done. The place was busting up. Too many despised each other when they weren't fornicating. It was like the country that way. Each faction did what it could to humiliate the others. The Oklahoma Hill Country faction called me to a meeting once and made me wait for hours. Nobody showed up. No whips, no chains, no torture device. Nothing like that. Just abandonment.

Without Frankenstein to keep a tentative peace in place, self-appointed bigwigs in the community thumped their Bibles with a vengeance. Uncle Faust grabbed his bald head with both hands, screamed to the skies in frustration and disgust—"Fuck fuck shit piss goddamn!"—and quoted Mark Twain to the delusional ones with the regressive cortexes. "It ain't those parts of the Bible that I can't understand that bother me; it is the parts that I do understand."

They screamed back at him "Abraham this" and "Isaac that," gibberish about taking all of us from up north to the mountaintop to slice us open, sacrificial lambs in God's name. "Abraham and Isaac?" Faust said. "A guy takes his kid to the mountaintop and plans to stab him to death? That's a homicidal psychopath in anybody's language."

"You can say that again," I said, and we packed our bags. North Dakota nice, we call it. Everybody in Fargo tells me Tulsa is paradise on Earth, with honest law enforcement, clean streets, and good work to be had—Woody Guthrie country. I don't tell them otherwise, since I didn't live in Tulsa itself, just in the hill country with a group of Bible-thumpers. All I want in the world is to do some good. So Tulsa is still on my pilgrimage map, still someplace to try when I need a change. When some yahoo tells me Tulsa is paradise, though, I wink and smile. "Is that the way it is?" I say. "If you go down that way, do it in a convoy. Dangerous days to travel alone. Don't take any guff from the swine with their Bibles." That's good advice I gave them. Tulsa's not the shithole Faust says it is—he's prejudiced because Bibles and attempted murder in the name of Abraham give him a rash—but it's no paradise, either, I can guarantee you that. No place on Earth is paradise. But then again, I've never been there. Not yet, anyway.

Nothing in America is a paradise, not anymore. It's just a place to get up each morning and do something to stay alive. Unless you're Frankenstein or Faust, who have a mission to instruct, improve, and entertain. "I'll give you a good laugh," they like to boast. And often they do. "Want a laugh?" It's one of their catchphrases. Not much to laugh about these days. "Want a laugh? Come listen. Come see."

Back in Fargo, punch-drunk after the commune, I rented a beat-up one-bedroom flat a short bus ride from the bombed-out civic center. I lived next to an alt girl whose actual God-given name, she claimed, was Cinderella. "Call me Cindy," she said, smiling. We had a smoke now and then, but she came and went according to a clock in her head whose workings I never figured out. You'll hear her story by and by.

It was autumn. The hawk of winter was on the move and would descend soon enough with a swoosh into the upper Midwest. But it was Indian summer, and that meant everybody was outside, mingling during the latest pandemic, many of them refusing to wear masks or keep their distance.

Faust and I settled into our routines while we waited for Frankenstein. While Faust went about his business, I sat and thought deep thoughts in a dark room to keep my mind, which is on the spectrum, from dissolving into a pudding of panic and waited for Frankenstein's soon return.

We worked on logistics. It would be a kind of talk show, we decided. Like the old days, Faust said on Skype. Frankenstein, preparing to leave the border but still tending to children in cages, flickered in and out of view on the monitor like a wraith. He looked grizzled like a town drunk, but his bright eyes were sharp and clean. He gave a thumbs-up, the nails bright with rainbow-colored lacquer, one of his trademarks, but uncut and gritty from hard labor.

He disintegrated into static. A wraith, indeed.

"How'd he decide on that name?" I asked Faust.

"Frankenstein, you mean? He used to have a car that was made out of body parts, or body parts made from an automobile, or a broken body put together with duct tape. Or something like that. Am I making any sense?"

I let it go. It was too much for me. I went home and drew the curtains to collect myself. Darkness helps me think. The light can be good when I need stimulation, but too much light and my brain burns.

In Fargo I wore tattered jeans and a shirt with a hole wherever I went. I wore an unzipped winter fleece whenever the hawk of winter waved its wings just to let us know where we were at. The shirt had a caption on it: "Stay Positive but Don't Test Positive." I often wore a wool cap to hide my big ears.

It was a grand day, warm and brisk, when Frankenstein returned dressed in jungle camouflage gear like an Army Ranger. He even packed heat in a holster on one hip; the pistol made a dent in his jiggling belly. He was made of fiberglass or plastic and not flesh. He winked at both of us when we came up to give him a hug and help him with his duffel bags, but held out a hand to keep us back. "I might be contagious," he said. "Give it a few days." He smelled like the border—a mix of scat and cactus, of eucalyptus rot with an efflorescence of javelina piss baked into his skin. He had the shakes. He didn't look too good. He'd have to fake it. If he could. I began to have my doubts.

They didn't rehearse. They had faith in their long game. "We always go long, never short," Faust liked to say. In his glory days, Frankenstein had interviewed everybody from Vice President Taylor Swift in the days before she became a politician—when she was a singer who starred in the musical remake of the movie *Fargo*, now officially classified as a national treasure—to Dan the Man, a stumpy, bald-headed cynic who loved to mock others. His own talk show, *Bumper Cars*, had gone bust when he developed his own affliction, not Tourette's but something that resembled it—an epidemic on the Northern Plains for a time—and went haywire on the airwaves. As for Faust, he had played with a limping Tiger Woods before the crippled golfer's assassination, and as a young man had drunk mescal with Joaquín "El Chapo" Guzmán. "Nice guy when he's in the right mood," he liked to say. "He threw a mean curve when we played sandlot ball." Then he hitched his star to Frankenstein, and the rest is history.

On the day of the show, the bus I took smelled like a urinal and perspiration and rotting potatoes. The clouds promised rain or snow. The temperature was dropping; I wore a dark fleece for comfort and camouflage. The big-bellied bus driver, chain-smoking through a soiled mask with a round hole in it for the cigarette, disregarded his "No Smoking" sign. He wore a green-and-yellow shirt that said "BISON" in big letters. The bus seats were slit. Filthy fibers of cotton stuffing clung to my shirt and filled the bus with a wet, soiled stink.

The streets were quiet until we got downtown. We rattled past a bank. I saw the glint of marble floors. Helmets on square heads, lots of automatic rifles. It wasn't a bank, I realized, but a bar that had once been a bank. The bus ground to a halt, its brakes on their last legs, and stopped a block past the bar at the burnt-out hulk of a building that had once housed the local newspaper, now defunct. The driver, in no hurry, stared at a gang of punks dressed in red jackets with decals of fire-breathing dragons. "It's a great day to be a dragon!" they shouted in unison. They were beating up an old codger with his own cane; he was so stooped that he tried inching away from them like a crab.

"Spring training," one of the punks shouted toward the bus, as if challenging any of us to intervene. "This is it for the old coot!" *Coot*, I thought; *I haven't heard that word in a week of Sundays*. I made a note of the word. The punks dragged the coot along, his body limp but twitching spasmodically. "You can't do this to me!" he croaked. "Don't you know who I am?" His mask had been torn asunder, and blood spittle streamed down his face. The leader of the pack, with a swastika carved into one lobe of his shaven head, faced the bus—none of them were masked, of course—and curled his arms to show tattooed skin and muscle. He held out a branding iron; I could see the swastika burning bright. It was the new symbol of what we were all about, another reason some of the world treated American borders like prison walls.

Near the civic center, the curbs were cluttered with fast-food rubbish and small fires burning in the chill as the forsaken homeless tried to keep themselves warm. A man about my age, his chin bouncing on his chest, rode an adult tricycle in circles, shouting, "What's good for the goose is good for the baba ghanoush!" The civic center itself was a wreck. Piles of plaster, air that tasted of mold and mildew, beggars holding out their cups but cringing at any sudden move. The governor had approved legislation that authorized any legal to shoot any illegal or indigent for any reason at all, so long as it was videotaped for required broadcast on local news.

Inside the arena, the air was electric, pumped full of intravenous drugs, offered at the door. The drugs promised immunity and allowed masks to be removed. Contrary, I kept mine in place and sat on a metal chair, my phone in my hand so I could communicate with Faust, who would wear an earplug onstage. A stoop-shouldered man with snow-white hair tapped my shoulder. "Hey, buddy," he said, "the guys with berets? They cops?" There were lots of them near kiosks that sold booze and drugs. They had on green berets and red armbands. A few carried rifles. Some were dressed like Vikings.

"No. They call themselves Militias," I said. "Vigilantes, but sometimes they keep the peace." Contemptuous, he pointed at people across the aisle on plyboard bleachers who wore costumes: men and women in hoop skirts, ex-vets in battle fatigues with big placards: "SUPPORT THE RIGHT TO ARM BEARS." The vigilantes with the berets and the purple Viking helmet with horns looked none too pleased. "No, I mean them hooligans," he said.

I smiled. This had to be one of Faust's pranks. "Hey," I said, "I'm on your side. Thumbs-up, buddy."

"Fucking A," he said, and popped me a crisp one on the shoulder that would hurt for two weeks. He told me his name. I told him mine and tightened up when he asked the inevitable question. "Heimlich? How that spelled? What it mean? You can save me if I start to choke?" I said anything that came to mind, secretly smug. Ninety-nine percent of the men in today's America have a sperm count too low to make babies, especially if they're unvaccinated; he was clearly one of them.

The production crew placed the guests on the sagging plywood stage. An end-of-the-world prophet. An impressionist in whiteface and rouge with a neon tattoo implanted in his chest: THOU SHALT, it read. A senile mystic with a turban covering his baldness—the whole world seemed to be going bald—and an oxygen tube in his mouth. It was the geriatric ward, the last of the boomers making a stand. *Thank you, boomers*, I wanted to shout.

But refrained.

The show started on schedule, but lights flickered and squeaking swamp fans stopped and started. Faust hurried on stage using crutches, one of those guys you admire because you know that before his arthritis turned his fingers into claws, he could play any instrument, including the tuba, but now he had the affliction of the body and the mind. He told us that special generators installed for the occasion provided absolute insurance against power failures.

"Hello, Fargo!" he shouted. He cupped a hand to one hear. "Let's hear it, Fargo! One. Two. Three: WHAT'S GOOD FOR THE GOOSE IS GOOD FOR THE BABA GHANOUSH!"

The ones in the crowd who recognized the signature sentence went wild.

"Fucking A," I said into my phone, set on loud volume, and saw him jerk at the sound but then laugh and stare out, searching for me and pointing an index finger my way as if it was the barrel of a gun.

Some in the crowd threw apple cores and even rotten eggs at him. The place was half full. All age groups. All status brackets. A suit here or there. Lots of team shirts and letter jackets. Some waved American flags. Some used sound makers that manufactured loud Bronx cheers.

Shots rang out.

One winged Faust in the foot. He screamed "Fuck!" then gave it up and motioned to the mystic with the turban and oxygen tube to warm up the crowd. A crew member came on stage with a first-aid kit.

Some of the berets and Vikings made their way into the audience and startled the complacent shooter, who apparently thought that anything goes. They approached him from behind, grabbed him by the shoulders, disarmed him, and dragged him to a fate that I didn't want to imagine. Later, it wouldn't surprise me if his mortuary pic showed up on the internet.

The mystic was a contortionist. He threw a tie-dyed sheet over his back and limped across the stage carpet, pretending to be Faust and gurgling incoherent omens into the mike.

"Boot out da bum!" somebody screamed. The mystic lost his temper, walked to the impressionist with the neon tattoo on his chest, and spit in his face. The impressionist waved, forgetting in his hipster senility how to move his arms, and accidentally slapped himself in the face, the gesture sufficiently comic to keep the angry patrons in their seats. Faust, his foot now bandaged by medics so practiced they could work the front lines of the latest brushfire war, brushed the gob of spit from the impressionist's painted face. He wagged a finger at the mystic. "Fucking stop it! Where's your decorum?" Then two goons in funny skirts waddled from backstage and dragged the mystic away, just in time for Frankenstein to make his entrance. "WHAT'S GOOD FOR THE GOOSE," he shouted, "IS GOOD FOR THE BABA GHANOUSH!"

I couldn't believe this was happening in Fargo, North Dakota, where courtesy was once king. Frankenstein himself didn't look too good. His head twitched from the residue of a minor stroke that had occurred earlier in the week. He was also contagious, so he wore a double mask that covered part of his baba ghanoush beard. He tried to do one of his classic monologues but forgot what he was saying and hid behind his mask and beard as if it was a shrub. "These lights," he muttered, nervously arranging notes.

"What the hell?" I said into my phone. This was not the Frankenstein I knew and loved. "Get him off the stage or bring him a glass of water," I said to Faust, who didn't appear to hear me in the hubbub. Or had he lost his earpiece in the fracas?

The place was filled with screaming human primates baying like hyenas; it reminded me of the tournaments where two or more fighters go at it until only one stands. Frankenstein knew what had happened to that rock star—what was his name, the one with the hair that never stopped?—who came to sing in Fargo but was literally torn to pieces when his voice froze up at the wrong time.

An egg splattered near the desk in the middle of Frankenstein's monologue. The monologue wasn't funny. I said so into my phone. Faust pointed at me and nodded to show he could hear. The egg wasn't a joke, either, though the audience broke into guffaws. Better than a bullet in the foot. Faust cut the whole thing short, limping up to Frankenstein and pulling him to his seat behind his desk. It made me mad. Even the Boss would have problems with a crowd like this, if the Boss hadn't developed Parkinson's and could still sing.

"You fuckers!" Faust screamed in a frenzy. "Cut the crap right now! THIS IS BABA GHANOUSH TIME!"

I stood and screamed to let him know he had my support. "Hey, Faust, my man! I'm with you, man! Remember the Paradise Intentional Community!"

He startled at that and squinted into the audience. I made a fist and held my arm up high. He did the same. A portion of the audience joined us. It was a moment. I won't forget it. It was the penultimate time I would see him alive.

The mystic had bombed. The impressionist was senile. Frankenstein introduced the prophet, an authentic muscle man. He wore faded Levi's and a T-shirt without sleeves, so you couldn't miss those ancient biceps as gnarled and strong as tree roots, like an old surfer with skin leathery enough to make into boots. He flexed his arms and featured the word on the tee. COURAGE, it said. Girls in nothing but G-strings came onto the stage and danced behind and around him, as if this was a performance by the late, great Pit Bull.

"Throw out da bum, I said!"

The two security guards on stage exchanged glances. They were unarmed and worried. One searched for the berets and the Viking helmets, who were still outside doing whatever they were doing to the guy who'd shot Faust's Achilles tendon.

"I'm a goodwill ambassador," Frankenstein had said, explaining why his security was unarmed. "Ambassadors don't pack six-shooters." I wondered what he had done with his pistol; he might need it. Enough is enough. We all know what happened to the rock star. How many national treasures can we afford to lose?

I hoped the prophet would be good, because the crowd was going ape. The prophet raised a hand for silence and cocked his head at a weird angle. He held out his chest. You could imagine him standing in a thunderstorm on a mountain in Tibet. He formed a temple with his fingers and bowed to the audience.

"Praying for peace?" Faust quipped.

"You want to know about the future?" he said, arms now flexed, the COURAGE on his tee almost glowing. "I'm afraid there's nothing but a blob on the horizon."

"Is it made of whipped cream?" Faust quipped again. "I heard some dairy cows were milked during an earthquake." Nobody laughed. Frankenstein, recovering his aplomb, raised his eyebrows and cupped a trembling, misshapen hand over one ear. Everyone groaned predictably. He relaxed.

I didn't. I had never seen him in such bad shape.

The prophet seemed oblivious to the ruckus. He pulled out a scarf from someplace and draped it over one shoulder, the kind of item you get from the local dollar store. "America must repay its psychic debts ... debts ...," he said. The echo amplified his powerful timbre. "Your karma is overloaded; you carry it all on your back, an albatross. I see a corpse dripping blood from its mouth. I see refugee families dying of thirst in the desert; I see pink mucus mutants crawling from your cellars, your attics, fastening to your throats like leeches. I see

71

an infestation of rats. I see another virus become another plague. I see women forced to bear babies sold into slavery. It happens again and again. It never stops. It's the Never-Ending Virus." He had the audience under his thumb. He had once been a member of the ruling party before seeing the light and converting to Chrislam, the new, hot religion. "The strobe lights of tracers," he said, "the napalm, the quick fix of a mushroom cloud. Seawater taking over the land. A virus in every pot of soup. Everyone a terrorist. A vast bloodletting. The Earth shedding its humans like vermin. Back to the source: the trees, the bugs, the vermin, the amoeba."

The crowd started getting pissed at his deranged Debbie Downer schtick, and I could only hear part of what he said. It was social media and conspiracy theory brought to life. "Hijacked missiles, blowtorches, pocket computers wired to bombs, firestorms, children turned to cinders, pain, pain, pain. Pedophiles everywhere! In every pizza box! You'll love it, lap at it like the dogs you are, do the dirty to your own kids, false pleasures, the Dark Age of the psyche. This country has no inward motion. All is lost!"

"Throw out da goddamn bum!" That crazed voice again. You could see Frankenstein turn pale at his desk. He rubbed his eyes. He frowned down at his notes. When he looked up again, his eyes grew wide like bowling balls.

A thing as much ape as man charged down the aisle. It had on a faded John Deere cap and overalls and waved a tiny red-white-and-blue flag. Under the overalls was a red-and-gold sweatshirt that featured an embossed ear of corn. "Lemme at him!" the ape screamed. "You traitor! Lemme at him!"

"Go get him, ya big Cobber!" the guy next to me shouted, ripping off his own shirt. There was a flag tattooed on his chest. Red. White. Blue.

"To hell with that," a woman behind me shouted. She wore a faded Frankenstein tee from the old days. I swiveled to see her whale the

72

guy with her heavy purse the size and shape of a watermelon. There must have been bricks in it. The guy dropped like a shot and lay still. She gave me a thumbs-up sign. "Go Faust!" she shouted. "Go Frankenstein!" She held out a hand to high-five me. I complied, my eyes on the purse.

The ape roared past us like freight. "Ya bum! It's all over!" I couldn't tell if it was half human, half ape, or what. A mutant of some kind. It had enough hair for the zoo. Jesus God Almighty, I thought, get Frankenstein and Faust to a safe place; even the border would be better than this. Good God in heaven, not them too. "Abort, abort!" I cried into my phone. "Abort!"

The berets and Viking helmets were back. They pulled out night-sticks and charged into the bleacher crowd. A few in the crowd with more brawn than brain splintered plyboard seats for weapons. I heard gunshots. A beret went down. The others opened fire.

The ape gathered momentum.

Some kid with a pistol stepped into the aisle to face the creature approaching him and took aim. The gun went off. But the creature, even with a blossom of blood on a shoulder, didn't stop. He trampled over the kid, stopping to stomp on his head, left him lying like a log in the aisle. On the edge of the stage a guard had aligned himself with the center aisle. He crouched in a three-point stance and braced himself. "Hup! Hup!" he screamed, muscles tight as a firing pin. I remembered that he had once been a tackle on the local Bison football team.

"Da bum's through!" the creature yelled. The guard leaped into its flailing fists. Their delirious screams were wonderful to hear for some, I could tell—a true catharsis, like the slow-motion metal-on-metal wrench of a car wreck. The crowd brawling near the stage stopped fighting for a moment to watch. Frankenstein was trying to hustle the prophet away. It was just like him, to think of others first, the compassionate pilgrim in Africa or on the border giving his all for the cause, but it was too late. The prophet, as if atoning for his Neanderthal opinions in the old language times, ripped off his T-shirt to expose his neon tattoo, which read "THOU SHALT NOT," and gave the brawling crowd some sort of farewell blessing before his head exploded. Then someone hit the fuses.

If this is a stupid pet trick, I thought, remembering the long-ago heyday of David Letterman, it's not working.

Imagine watching a program on the tube, sipping on a brew, maybe snuggling up to your Molly (may she rest in peace). Then you're inside the tube, with some goon pointing a bazooka at your head. By the time I stumbled out of the civic center, where pandemonium was still raging, sirens and gunshots filled the air and there was a light dusting of snow on the streets. It was below the freezing point, approaching the doughnut hole, zero Fahrenheit; I zipped up my fleece and my teeth still chattered.

The burned-out hulk of a bus was smoking. I hit the pavement, flattened myself against a building whenever a car or group of punks cruised by. Behind me a helicopter took off. Maybe that was Frankenstein and Faust, getting out alive, I thought, though it turned out not to be so. The rotors faded away into the heavens, and I lost faith.

Nobody gets out alive. It's time, I thought, to try Tulsa, to do some good there.

I stumbled over an unconscious man, blood all over his body, his face the color of caulk. It was the shooter from inside who had zinged Faust in the foot. The berets had done him over good. The body, dead I now realized, appeared to be turning white, but it was only the snow.

A midget in an Elmer Fudd cap stepped from the shadows near the body and shifted a brick from hand to hand. "Terrible, ain't it?" he said. "They kicked him in the ribs. Put a rifle butt in his face. Then the knife, zooie." He spit and paused to breathe heavy. "Watcha doing on the streets dis time a night, by the way?"

"Walking to my karate class. Black belt. Hands that can kill."

He slapped one of his own hands onto my shoulder. "Why don't cha stop for a sec? Look, here's my problem," he said. He wasn't wearing a mask. "I got cancer. It hurts, you know? I need some comfort." He rubbed his hand on my upper thigh and winked. "I like Marines, and Marines sure as hell like me. You ever been a Marine?"

An old battered Buick screeched around a corner, nearly lost control on the slick, wet asphalt, and braked at the curb. A crew of thugs in ducktails, leather jackets, and pointed boots whooped out like vampires. They swung tire chains and machetes and baseball bats. Each had on a beret or an armband. "There's the dwarf!" one screamed.

He took off. A greaser blew the horn twice. They all piled back in the car and somebody who looked like Faust stuck his head out the window. "You can run, you fucking dwarf, but you can't hide!" He saw me, winked, and gave the thumbs-up.

That was about it.

Back home I turned on the tube. So what if the world figures America is a wreck that needs a tow? More room for you and more room for me. Some sort of accident, the newscaster claimed. Something big blew up and the Pacific Northwest territory is entirely radioactive. It wasn't deliberate, the president said, but hey, shit happens. He clicked his bottle of Coca-Cola against the camera, a close-up, and wrapped a shoulder around a stuffed grizzly bear standing tall on its hind legs in his nuclear-safe hideaway inside a mountain.

So what if illegals were dying by the thousands on account of the new law? Women being flailed with whips for disobedience? If the Cold War had turned hot? Frankenstein and Faust, coming out of retirement, that was the real news, but Frankenstein's obituary would be tomorrow's sidebar, wouldn't it? The late Mr. Frankenstein, part of that great comedy club in the sky, all his body parts returning to the source, giving it all up, like Jesus, sacrificing his own life to redeem us all.

And global warming? An afterthought. Fake news.

What global warming? When I stare from my window, everything is white and clean. It's damned cold up here this time of year.

There's got to be something better than this. Tulsa, here I come.

PART TWO
Sharp Objects

Dark Times

The family of six reached the shotgun shack at dusk. "Oh, my God," said Sharon, who was six. Tina, her mother, once a homecoming queen, now having one of her typical bad days, didn't react. Her breathing sounded shallow.

"Yuck!" the two older kids screamed in unison. The infant started to bawl.

Tom, their father, laughed the sort of laugh designed to irritate his family to the edge of derangement. Once, he had played high school football with Chuck and played cornet in the school band, a double whammy that gave him a reputation as a Renaissance kid; those glory days were long gone. "Now, now, brown cow," he said. "What's good for the goose is good for the baba ghanoush." It was sadistic, he knew, to tease them like that, repeating nonsense stuck in his head, but he could see paint peeling from the cypress walls and needed to do something to break the spell of marital ennui. "That's good wood," he said.

79

Inside, the bed liner was worn. The place smelled like mothballs. An air-conditioning unit rattled in one window. A stream of water dripped from it, but the machine cooled the room, or at least kept the Mississippi Delta heat at bay.

"Oh, Daddy," Sharon said. "This is yucky. Why they call it a shotgun shack?"

"All the rooms and doors are one behind the next. If somebody shot a shotgun through the door, the shot would go all the way out back." Tom was manic. He unloaded suitcases from the car. His wife sat like a zombie on one of three double beds. What the hell. Each had bedspreads quilted together with squares that looked like fabric from an American flag. The shacks were not cheap, but Tom insisted on staying two nights for the atmosphere on the way to Orlando and Disneyworld. It was his treat to himself. Afterward, he would reunite with his role as a good family man and again become the religious zealot his wife now expected.

Lately, she was in a very dark place. That was one reason for the vacation, to get her out of the house and away from nosy Fargo neighbors, especially one who called Tom at work. "She needs help now. Now, Tom. Why aren't you doing anything?" Tom would excuse himself and ask his secretary to screen calls from the woman. He would telephone his wife at home and sweet-talk her for a few minutes. "I'm doing what I can for her," he explained to the doctor he consulted, one who put her on strong medication that she didn't always take. "We have the Bible. Scripture. The best medicine available."

The doc stared, his hands steepled and chin resting on his thumbs. "Make her take the pills, Tom. God helps those who help themselves."

The shack had a tin roof. Later that evening, they sat at a wooden table in the kitchen eating barbecue Tom had brought back from a take-out place and juke joint up the road. A rainstorm passed. They heard clatter on the tin roof. It was the strangest sound. "Like a new kind of music," Tom said. He was delirious with happiness, despite the bawling of the infant and his wife's catatonia. Sharon was the only one interested in his stories about great bluesmen like Robert Johnson, who sold his soul to the devil just down the road.

With a finger, Sharon traced the numbers on the license plate that covered a hole in the wall. Though the place was quaint—a nice word for it—and reservations had been difficult to get, only his six-year-old daughter appreciated it. "You're Daddy's girl," Tom said. She lay her head in his lap and he stroked her long golden hair. After a time, she slept. He carried her to a bed and lay her down next to her sister, who had crawled under the covers on her own. He wiped Sharon's fingers, still greasy from barbecue, and eased off her underpants, did his best to Velcro a plastic diaper into place.

The baby had cried herself to sleep. The oldest, Ben, had claimed the bed in the back room and closed the door. Tom knocked, reminded him to read his Scripture, and said goodnight. There was nothing left now except the patter of rain and his wife's guttural yelps.

"What's that?" Tom asked. She had refused to eat ribs, stared at them as if they were crawling with maggots.

"They're unclean," she said. She ate cereal instead. Cornflakes were scattered on the cypress floor around her.

He swept them up with a piece of cardboard. "You all right?"

She said nothing. He went to the suitcase and foraged for her medicine. He fingered out a dose and offered the pills with a glass of water. She stared up at him. Once, he might have reached over, touched her, but that time had passed. The growing dystopia in the world around them paled in comparison to his marriage and its gloom. Any contact made her flinch. She had become depressed when the infant came with God's glory into the world and couldn't—or wouldn't, Tom suspected, out of sheer obstinacy—snap out of it.

"Look, honey," Tom said, too manic to sit for long, "there's a juke joint down the road. Mind if I take in a set?" Blues music was his vice.

He admitted as much, but had promised himself a taste on the way to Orlando. He would put it behind him soon enough.

She munched cornflakes one flake at a time, taking two or three bites from each flake. He brought over a bedspread made from American flags and draped it over her shoulders. "Red white and blue / Just for you," he crooned. "I won't be long, maybe an hour. Get some sleep."

He was gone two, maybe three hours. He usually didn't drink, but he had a few. He had a good time in a joint full of tourists and local people with accents so thick he could barely figure out what they said. The music was fantastic. It took him away from himself. The wailing guitar, the deep throbbing bass, the throaty syllables more like a growl than a voice. Some of the locals carried guns in holsters on their hips, but it felt right to him, like atmosphere, authenticity. He could tell that everybody in the place understood how much he loved the blues.

How could something so good be a blasphemy? He would have to do some debting the next day, he reminded himself, pray without cease as he drove to Florida to pay back the Good Lord for tonight's good times. Fair enough.

Outside the juke joint, the rain had moved on and the night was clear, the sky full of stars.

A God-given sky.

When Tom pulled into the gravel drive next to the shack, he was still humming songs and didn't see his wife until he was upon her. She sat, almost invisible, on the crooked front steps, moving her fingers together as if sewing with needle and thread.

Tom tumbled from the car, stood stock still under the stars. He set his mouth and walked to her. "Can't sleep?" His happiness felt too good to waste. I married the homecoming queen, he thought, and this is what it comes to. He wanted to crawl under the red-white-and-blue bedspread and dream bluesy dreams.

"My babies are gone," she said.

"What?"

She repeated the words.

He felt the chill like the sound of a train whistle down the tracks, like the week of riots in Fargo that had burned down a dozen houses (one of them just down the block from his own), the wail of a blues guitar howling in the wind (like a voice hoarse from singing the blues). The crackle of the blues could take you down and down to the bottom of things. Which was where he sometimes felt he belonged.

In the shack, the first thing he saw was Sharon's hair, cut from her head and lying like golden weeds on the bed's white pillow. Beautiful hair, he thought, rotating his neck absentmindedly to clear his head.

She was in the bathtub, dead in water the color of blood.

His other children, also dead, lay naked on the double beds. They were propped like mannequins into grotesque positions, arms and legs splayed. His son, apparently still alive, had crawled to the floor before dying, leaving a trail like bloody snail slime.

He could hear the thrum of the guitar and made a smacking, hungry sound, though he wasn't aware that he was doing so. In his head, in the dark, he could hear blues from the juke joint miles down the road but couldn't tell if it was a song coming to a glorious end or just beginning to assert itself among the ruins.

He, Like, Died

I wanted Heimlich to help me when it happened, when I found out I was in deep shit, but he had lit out for Tulsa, I heard, or someplace like that, and I tried to explain it the right way, the way he might have done, but it came out all wrong, didn't it?

* * *

Look, officer, it was raining. A heavy rain, for Chrissakes. That's the first thing. You ever drive in that part of town at that time of night in a storm? Yeah, lightning, thunder, the whole ball of wax. And yeah, the stories you hear are true. I was high, why deny it, sweetcakes? Dee Dee was high as a kite. I'm a lady most of the day, work as a nurse's aide in the senior center full of Q-tips, I'm damn good too, and that's not just me talking, counselor. You can look at performance reports any damn time you want. I wear the mask, take the pills, follow every regulation. Even when the riots came after Frankenstein was killed, I drove to the center every day for my shift, even got carjacked once but trudged through the snow to punch the clock, that's me to a T.

That night, though, that night I'd gone to a powwow rave, and what's one of them without a tab? Of what? Of Ecstasy, counselor, pure love. You're a counselor, right? You've read me my rights?

And during the party, I didn't count the drinks. What? Oh, mostly vodka, I think, though I drank a lot of H_2O too. I'm not a nurse's aide for nothing. I'm no novice, so don't get that look. Fact is, I felt all right in the car, but like I said, it was a bad part of town. You know what it's like out there these days; you can't stop for hell or high water. I was drunk, and high, and this godawful rain like golden crystals was on the windshield. Snow with sleet, both at the same time.

I forgot to turn the wipers on. And there he was, swear to God, in the street, stumbling, drunk. I didn't know what the fuck it was, thought he might be a Marauder armed to the teeth. A living nightmare. And I hit him. Or he walked into the bumper, actually, and I must have been going fast, because he got stuck in the windshield.

Stuck, I say. Can you believe that shit?

What? Headfirst. Part of his head was like in the car with me. Maybe the windshield was already cracked; yeah it actually was, because how else could most of his head end up inside my personal space? He moaned, was like really stuck. I like freaked when I came to myself—did I tell you the crash knocked me out?—with this flea-bitten head in my personal space. He was breathing on me; I wasn't wearing no mask, and he was bleeding. I veered from side to side to get him out of my car. That's when I sideswiped that Buick.

Hey, see it from my perspective. I had no idea what to do, so I drove him to my house and parked in my garage. I wouldn't be sitting here now in this stupid jailhouse if Serena, that bitch I thought was my pal, hadn't called the goddamn cops and snitched. What made her do that? Snitch the Bitch. I'll have her killed, counselor. If anything happens to me. You know I will.

Can I have a smoke, counselor? You don't? Well, fuck; what the fuck are you good for then? Well, what the hell; this is one of them new places anyway, and I'm not supposed to smoke. Got to go to the exercise yard. So you're saving us both a lecture. Thank you, counselor.

Right. Okay. Well, this tramp, maybe I read in the news he was forty or something ancient like that, looked one hundred, was stuck in my windshield, bleeding all over the dashboard. I mean, don't get me wrong. I wasn't happy; I didn't ask the guy to step into my car to hitch a free ride, but that day it wasn't the biggest thing on my mind. I apologized and told him he could just walk out of my life and save us both a ton of trouble, but he had one eye pierced by the glass he went through. Damn glass is supposed to be shatterproof. Shatterproof, my ass. And he was like, well, I don't know, stuck.

I mean, I apologized. "I'm sorry," I said.

"Help me," he said, or I think that's what he gurgled, but I couldn't handle it. I mean, what was I supposed to do, counselor? He had long funky hair matted with something that stunk like shit. Puke, maybe? Matted blood? Yukky shit. Or maybe that cotton candy shit that comes out of your head? And you want to know the goose that's good for the baba ghanoush? I thought I recognized him under all the shit. He used to do talk shows on TV before it hit the fan. You know who I mean, right? God, I wish I had Heimlich here. Remember him? He remembers everything. Like a raven. Ravens never forget, counselor. You know that, right? He would translate what I'm saying for you so you could understand my dilemma.

I went in the house and meant to help, but I was so goddamned anxious that I had a few pops and smokes and listened to a few tunes to calm my nerves; then I crashed in the crib and slept like a baby. I crashed, man, and the next day, or maybe it was even the one after that, I went out to the car to go get my smokes and freaked out when

I saw he was still in my garage, still stuck in the windshield. Not moving. I tell you true, counselor; I had forgot all about the dude, like a nightmare. Maybe I thought I was hallucinating. I was freaked like a bump on a lump of log. Post trauma, maybe that's my plea. I mean, all right, I'll say it straight: I was flat-out fucked up. I fucked up, all right? PTSD.

Am I in trouble? What, murder? Manslaughter? No, no way it's that. I mean, he, like, died, yeah, but I didn't do nothing to him. He just, like, jumped in my car headfirst, and after a while he died. I went out there the third or fourth day to see if he had crawled off when his head lost some weight and he could get loose. The passenger seat was soaked, counselor. If I was about killing the dude, don't you think I would have washed it off to hide the evidence?

Anyway, the dude was cold and stiff. It freaked me. And he stunk. Like a skunk.

So I left him like that but, I mean, don't they rot after a while? I started worrying there might be a smell or something or that the dude's spirit might be in pain or stuck. I called my friends, the good ones, I mean, not Snitch the Bitch that got me in this mess, and they came over and said, "My God, Dee Dee, what have you done?"

They bitched at me, but after I explained how fucked up I was and made a big pot of red-hot chili with cheese and bought a case of beer, they came around. We put the guy—or his body, I guess I should say, right?—in the trunk of another car—no, not the Buick—and dumped him in that park by the Red River. You know the one I mean? Gooseberry, right?

And that would be that. What's done is done, right? You can't bring back the dead; but I tell you, if I was Jesus, I would help the guy. Like Lazarus. Remember him? He came back from the dead. Good as new. This guy? No way, counselor. Dead. For good.

They found the body, I guess. I don't read papers or watch news, so I take your word, but nobody connected me to it, and it never,

never would happen again. I ain't no murderer, nothing like that, but I got drunk with Snitch the Bitch and told her the story for no real reason, just because, and you got to admit this, it *is* a good story to tell—a brush with death, that kind of thing; a man tries to carjack your ride and gets himself trapped like a wolf that can only get back into the brush if it gnaws off its leg.

But I guess you can't gnaw off your head that way, because how can you take out your teeth to get at your neck? I even told her that when we dumped the body, we said a prayer for it, me and my friends, and that was truth; I didn't make that shit up. Doesn't that show I'm not bad? We even laid him to rest, but Snitch the Bitch took it with her and told it to the cops, and so now I'm busted.

If that's what this is.

Hard to believe, the way things go these days, that you're busting me over some little thing. Don't we all have bigger problems? Like climate change and flooding and tornadoes and all those Marauders who do as they please? Why me? WHY ME?

So, yeah, I fucked up. Call me guilty, but it was a freak accident. They really gonna make a crime of it? Can I just apologize, pay for the dude's coffin? I mean, if they want me to show I'm sorry.

How much would that be, do you think? I mean, am I in trouble? Am I really in trouble, counselor? Or is that just you kidding around to make me feel bad?

Getting Even

There was a smell of ozone after a rain in Fargo that August afternoon, Cinderella told Heimlich, where distemper came to rule, in the days before he relocated to Tulsa, a work in progress, but more peaceful than not most days, where he now had what he called a home—a place to stay where he could be of use to others, but he remembered that he wasn't of much use, if any, to Cinderella.

Cinderella—"Call me Cindy" was her perpetual mantra—in the story she told him, wore headphones, riffing to private music as she walked two small dogs along the river. She didn't hear the man on the racing bike until too late. The big man biked fast, followed sharp turns on the rain-slick walk as though a contestant racing against himself. The glisten of sweat on his calves was a detail she described in her hospital haze to doctor and cop, both in hazmat suits, which surprised her. She was concussed, fuzzy, but thought the virus had run its course once the vaccine was administered.

New virus, one said.

The biker had on a T-shirt, rust-colored sweats, she said, or maybe the sweats were indigo blue. The bicycle was rust too. A bully, a boor, a jerk, she thought but didn't say, perhaps conflating the biker with a former lover who had treated her like shit. No prince, anyway.

Beatific, she thought the doctor said, but that wasn't right. She thought she saw him give the cop a sardonic stare, maybe roll his eyes. She squinched her own eyes against the glare.

The memory played in slow motion, she told Heimlich.

A raking bike, she said to the cop. "You mean racing?" he said, leaning close. His eyes glinted inside the face shield.

"Yes, raked me over. Head-butted, crushed ribs, flipped me. Like a pancake. Just like a pancake. Or waffle. Then went at my crotch. He was Hemingway. I have the tapes," she said to the cop, praying he would move away from her—too close, too damned close—so she could stop holding her breath, but the doctor listened too, and later a lawyer from the DA's office, also in hazmat attire. She repeated everything.

"Hemingway?" The cop stood. His equipment clanked like a machine that needed oil. He gave the doctor another stare. They didn't believe her.

"Yes, works in IT. Follows me wherever I go."

"You're saying the guy on the bike who assaulted you was this IT guy you know?"

"I remember that guy," Heimlich said, hearing the story. "A bully. I wish I had been there to help you translate."

As she lay on the path catching her breath, waiting for help, the back of her head soggy like muskmelon rind—talk and die, she recalled, head trauma—she heard the shriek of an afternoon freight clatter through town, the *clunk-clunk-clunk* of steel wheels on iron rattling her ribs, two of which, it turned out, were broken.

"Admit it," he said on the bike trail, assaulting her, one of his bike's wheels still spinning. "You want me so much, you want to be me."

Hearing the story, Heimlich felt his own bile rise.

She fell into a dream, feverish, thirsty, thinking of the nearby Red River with its green scum. The image of Hemingway on his bike gave way at the hospital to a memory. She tried not to say it; it made her sound woozy, stupid. "He put me in a vise," she said, "a brace made of metal and wood, concrete. It had a lever; a jaw opened and closed. He stretched his lips out thin. Big white teeth. He enjoyed my pain. A sadist. With his bike chain. He wanted to eat me. 'You're my sadist,'" he said. 'Start dominating.' I told him we were done. 'If you leave me,' he said, 'I'll shoot you.'"

She stopped. Time was tangled in her head. Cop turned to doc and shook his head. They were both men. What did she expect? One gave the other a male gaze. She didn't make sense, eyes cloudy, face hot with blood, and she didn't make much more sense when she told it to Heimlich. The man with the vise came from a dream she had after her abortion, nothing to do with Hemingway on the bike, but how to backtrack? How could they understand her pain? Hemingway, the man who made her pregnant, enjoyed pain. Or was that the IT guy? Were they one and the same? She gave up thinking and closed her eyes.

It was a sweltering afternoon. He biked so fast he couldn't stop, only he wasn't the IT guy until she remembered it in the hospital, with nurse and doctor, then doctor and cop, then cop and lawyer. "Look, Cinderella," the cop said; "I don't follow. Who's Hemingway? Who's IT guy? You're concussed."

"It's Cindy."

"Yeah, okay. Whatever. Cindy. Same questions. I'm trying to help here."

A relay race; she was the baton passed from one man to the next, one season of life to the next, walking two dogs, one a high-strung poodle named Wolf, the dog she hated yet now was hers, or she was responsible for it. The other, a schnauzer named Schnitzel, was a wiry miniature the color of salt and cinnamon. Both on leashes. She lived on a leash too, she tried to say to Heimlich, but he scratched his head and pulled at his hair, confused. Walking the dogs, she was caterwauling, songs without sense, just to hear her voice above the racket in her ears, coaxing each dog on the trail along the Red River to do its business so she could walk up the hill to the house where she sat over summer for owners stuck in Europe when the new pandemic struck. Whenever anyone asked—hardly ever—she said they were people who named a poodle Wolf and a schnauzer Schnitzel.

"I'm having trouble following you," Heimlich said, his own head jangly with a mild, chronic case of the virus. "You're conflating two experiences. Remember you told me the Marauders raped you and put you in an old rusted cage intended for bears? You think you might be getting what happened then tangled up with the bully you call Hemingway? Or with hallucinations? Nothing wrong with that, given what you've been through. But I'm woozy myself. I can't follow."

Ear-jangling music by a new alternative band, Noble Rot, in her ears. She believed they would break through. She wanted a strong drink with the vocalist's high-pitched wail, maybe a G&T or a buck-naked margarita. She worked on a computer terminal for the arts section of a weekly paper; gathered information, organized it, put it out, mostly just listing acts but sometimes reviewing. Her wrists were sore most nights, required medication. Some kind of condition, sore capillaries or something.

Carpal tunnel! That was it. Head injury! Lucky to be here. Isn't that what the doc told her? "Cinderella." He said her full name. Grinned it at her

"It's Cindy."

"No prince yet? No shoe that fits?" The doc smirked. Goddamn asshole.

A strong drink was the best medication. Hemingway—the writer, not her attacker—had called it the giant killer. She rather liked that, remembered it when she drank, remembered her aborted child, the IT impregnator who told her about Hemingway the

94

writer, whom he said he resembled, and made her pregnant and became Hemingway, name and all, by osmosis—a middle-aged IT guy with a gut who did IT stuff at the local university and had a reputation for bearing down on women until they did things they didn't particularly want to do. "I always get my way," he told her on their first date. "You should file that for safekeeping." She knew two women who had been involved with him. The three met once a year to drink and trade Hemingway stories. A kind of club. It kept all of them sane. Well, maybe the others didn't need it the way she did. They had partners; she didn't.

He cultivated a Hemingway mustache, the one the writer had. He was a big strapping boy in his mid-fifties. Maybe sixty. Full of literary fantasy, one woman said, still indignant. This IT guy who wrote on the side believed the corrupt establishment had not yet discovered him. He belonged in the pantheon with Joyce, Faulkner, Rushdie, Knausgård, those types. Cormac McCarthy. He liked to hold up the back cover of a Hemingway book and stare, studying himself as if staring into a mirror.

Heimlich just listened, biding his time, letting her talk. He could tell she had to get it all out, a kind of verbal constipation finally breaking loose like the crap after a virus that indicates one might be on the mend. He knew how to listen, he even thought, sometimes, that it was his superpower.

The other women laughed and clinked their beer steins with Cindy, who carried his image in her empty womb and knew she had to put him behind her. Such bitter thoughts and jangled music walking the dogs. Noble Rot would be in town, and she had a ticket—close to the front, middle-aged herself, surrounded by kids so young they might belong to her. None did.

The walk on the river would be pleasant without dogs. The cottonwoods and oaks and green ash, an occasional surviving elm, gave shade. Birds and squirrels, music and nature. She was almost happy, though she would feel the same if weeping. And it would be nice to be there without dogs.

She loved to weep, she told Heimlich. It gave her hope when tears stopped.

In middle age she was a weeper. It was her one indulgence. She had become one of those people who wept at movies. Tears trickled. She wiped them off when the child said "I love you" to the returning mother; when the husband, a philanderer, apologized and was forgiven as the house lights blazed in an empty theater. The men she met were too kind or not kind enough. Hemingway was never too kind, but then he was never kind enough. Two for one. Her men were mean after first dates. Maybe she brought it out in them with sarcastic wit, but only the IT guy who imagined himself Hemingway had made her pregnant, forced the abortion, given her a bouquet taken from the cemetery across the street from the clinic. Or was that somebody else? In the hospital, it was all a blur.

Just before the bike smashed into her, she smelled creosote and crepe myrtle, or some perfume, a scent released by the morning rain, cold enough to predict snow; or could it be a disinfectant used at the coal-fired electric plant whose white smokestacks and rusty water tower dominated the horizon?

Sweat dripped from his forehead as he came fast around the curve. He leered at her, his face stretched in a grimace of self-disgust. He had no control over the bike. Its front wheel, with a narrow gauge, wobbled. Schnitzel barked and pulled hard on the leash. She lost the leash but clung to Wolf's, took a step back, saw the man still pump the pedals, try to right himself. The pedals gleamed in the sun. She tried backing to higher ground and fell. Vertigo. He too lost control and, surrendering to fate, flew over handlebars as the day turned: fairy-tale weather, clear, chalky, the beginning of the long fog in her deepest brain, a different kind of shipwreck in a world filled with lost souls.

The jangling music a soundtrack. She couldn't remember lyrics. High mercury music. Wasn't that what somebody called it? He landed on top of her and she cried out. The back of her head thudded: concrete. Something gave. She blacked out. The bike clattered. A wheel spun and clicked as though a playing card clipped to it with a clothespin riffled in rhythm with the spokes.

Wolf yelped.

"Shit," Hemingway said. He moaned. "Goddamn bitch. Watch where you walk." He said it from some hollow place and buried his face in her crotch, her legs spread-eagled. He was topsy-turvy on her, as though prepared for cunnilingus. Was that the word?

In the hospital, the words came hard. She tasted his sweat, felt his nose tunnel into her crotch, searching for something lost, forgotten. He grunted. She was dazed on the bike path, thoughts like chalk. In the hospital they came clear. He was Hemingway, who made her pregnant—and raped her. The back of her head ached. She was nauseous with his weight, her pain. Somebody pried open her skull with a crowbar. She pushed him aside, retched, puked up bile, tasted its scent, groaned, tried to say "Get off." He dug into her, breathing hard, as though his nose was a penis and he would leave snot instead of seed.

Schnitzel was long gone, maybe home, maybe in the trees, but Wolf still yelped. He was all over Hemingway. He planted his nails in the man's back and jerked his pelvis against a strip of exposed skin, pale and visible where the T-shirt bunched. She could see the tail twitch and the dog's hindquarters rotate.

It could have been funny.

Heimlich tried to keep it all straight. She wasn't making it easy. The story jumped on him, coming from three directions at once. He wasn't even certain he knew who was who.

Hemingway pulled himself from her crotch with a groan, she told him, and reached behind for the dog. "So here we are," he mumbled, sitting up. "Together again. The happy couple." He tossed the dog like a plush toy to the bike path, where tiny nails clicked on wet pavement. It tried to run; its paws couldn't find purchase on concrete slick with perspiration and bicycle grease. It ran in place like a comic book imposter. Hemingway grabbed it and stood up holding it tight. It quivered and yelped in his muscled hands. All she could see was a ball of hair jerk and squirm in panic. He lowered his head, swung Wolf in half circles as though waltzing with it, then made a sigh, dropped it and sat on top of it as though it was a pillow. It yipped, once, twice—a muffled sound, asthmatic even—and then the cawing of a crow, grass keening in wind, labored breathing, and Noble Rot's tinny guitar riffs spilling insect-like from the headphone in the grass.

The world swung like a carnival ride. "Get up," she said, or thought she said, but it came out the way someone might mumble in sleep. The concussion was taking its toll.

"Up?" he said, staring. On his T-shirt a devil, some kind of Satan, was raping from behind a woman who wore a bonnet. She looked like Little Red Riding Hood. "Who's your daddy?" the devil asked in a balloon of dialogue. In the hospital she mentioned none of this, because Hemingway would not wear such an item of clothing, and it was Hemingway who had raped her, who had grunted into her crotch and raped her. The memory must be false.

"Didn't you hear me yell?" he said. "Didn't you hear me shout? I lost control. You didn't get the hell out of my way."

"Wolf," she gestured, too weak and dizzy to pull him off the dog. "You're sitting on Wolf."

The man frowned and wiped blood from his face, though she did not tell the doctor or detective about his blood. When he stood up, it was too late. The ball of fur had flattened on the sidewalk as though air had been let out of it.

"All the way to Granny's house," he said. "Big bad wolf."

"What? What was that?" She reamed out one ear with a bloody finger, opened and closed her eyes, and stared at the cattails beside the river, at the open sky.

"Did I kill big bad Wolf?" He picked it up, ruffled its fur, held it to his ear. "Hell of a thing." He said something in Latin and walked with the corpse to the cattails, tossed it into the river, and came back to her and sat down in Wolf's spot. "What do you think?" he said. "Should we say a prayer? Recite the rosary?"

"You're a killer," she said. "A goddamn killer. You'll pay." She could taste blood. "You raped me. You don't remember that?" She wondered if her ears dripped blood.

"I'll pay? Who's gonna make me? And for what? What did I do?"

"I'll make you pay."

"Oh yeah? You and who else?"

"Schnitzer, Schnitzel, Schnauzer," she said to the doctor. "Did they find the Schnitzel?"

"Lie down," the doc said. "Take it easy."

She took his advice and felt like she was swimming in her own blood. She could feel it pump like red ink, everything red and chalky except for Hemingway, the way you might remember a single actor in a movie but not the plot or other characters. This was not music, not high mercury sound. "Raped me," she mumbled. "Hemingway. IT. Hacked my phone."

"It's all right," the detective said. "We'll get it sorted. That's what we're here for." There was antiseptic in the room and a bandage she could feel on the back of her itchy head when she tried to scratch. The bedsheets were impossible, heavy as shrouds. She wanted to kick them off but couldn't. Why did everything take so much energy?

"What do I smell?" she asked.

She remembered that Hemingway had left her. "Look," he said, "I sat on it. I didn't know it was a dog. My mistake. *C'est la vie.*" She could remember her hysteria, but he disappeared. Walked away pushing the bike with the wobbly wheel.

Or maybe she disappeared, blacked out, and came to in the hospital bed to stare at a nurse. Had he brought her here? Where was Schnitzel? At least she had tapes, the record of what he did when he found out she was pregnant.

"Tapes," she said, nodding off, jerking awake, terrified. Head injury. Stay alert. But how long had she been in bed? Hours, days? Weeks? A coma?

She would get even with Hemingway. The tapes, answering machine tapes, messages from him full of threat, bluster. He lived alone, she knew that, and would have no alibi because he was guilty. He had no alibi, and she had the tapes. She had the tapes and he was guilty. It had to be true, because she remembered it with clarity.

"I know you're home, bitch," one tape said. "If I come over and knock and you don't answer, I'll huff and puff and break down your goddamn door. And then you'll be sorry as hell."

Big bad Wolf, she thought; *he killed the big bad Wolf.*

Heimlich listened but gave up trying to sort it. He let her talk. What did it matter if he understood? She could tell it again, until she had it straight. She could dream and wake to the memory. That was his job. To listen. The sun-fired summer with its sweats and bilious odors would give way to woodsmoke and morning frost. Powdery thoughts would blow away.

Clouds moved fast outside the window in the room where they both sat. He was already thinking ahead to the life he might make in Tulsa, if that's where he ended up.

PART THREE
In Transit

Fish Go Wild for the Swedish Pimple

To get to the fish house on the ice, Serena had to negotiate what felt like a gauntlet, a line of pickups and jeeps and cars stacked up waiting at the wintry resort to get on the ice like jets waiting on the tarmac for takeoff. The fish house belonged to an uncle, not the resort, but this access point was the one she knew. She hadn't seen him in years, didn't know if he was still among the living. There had been a falling-out between him and her Nana.

On the thick ice, streets had been plowed and road signs set up. No Marauders up in these parts, too damn cold. Too many local vigilantes and Militias. All hell might break loose if anybody had the audacity to mess with fish house culture. Walleye Lane, Jiggen Lane. Serena had a quick flash of her Nana doing a jig to cheer her up the night after she had scored her first righteous kill. Things had settled down some since that day. She still had the gun she had used, kept it oiled. She had used it since and would do so again if it came to that, but she wasn't looking for trouble. Sometimes, though, trouble came her way. This was a different kind of trouble.

Some fish houses were two stories tall. One had a chimney spewing smoke that smelled of bacon. Her stomach grumbled. She crunched over ice past the transient town to an unplowed section of lake, kept wiping the windshield because her defroster in the old pickup, the one that had belonged to Nana, didn't work the way it should. She clenched the steering wheel. Smoke belched from the exhaust. Her breath came in shallow gulps, but the truck's other passenger, bundled like fishing gear on the floor beside her, couldn't speak. Would never utter a word.

Udder, she thought, her breasts distended with milk. Udder. Mudder. Madre. Ava, she thought. My mother is a palindrome. It was a catchphrase she repeated too often for comfort.

The landscape astonished. She gulped; a salty tear froze on her face. In the past, on the lake with her boyfriend for a tryst in the fish house—a bottle of Kentucky bourbon half empty to make them forget how cold it was near the Canadian border as they drove on water in the mythical region known as Lake of the Woods, not so far from the Boundary Waters where her mother, Ava, had been taken long ago, never to return—she had stared hypnotized at the tree line miles away, lost in a fairy tale of romance about the pretty boy beside her, the sun sometimes sculpting the afternoon sky with twin rainbows, or sundogs, the wind whipping the air into a frenzy, the fish houses big or small dotting the tundra like a scene from one of the Grimm tales that her stern and abusive birth father had read to her once or twice when she was young. That was many years ago, when she had a father, so far as he went, only a comma in a long sentence, and her mother, Ava. She longed for Ava sometimes.

It's that kind of world, she thought with stoicism. She fishtailed into light snow next to the house. She fished out the key entrusted to her Nana by the uncle, a hunter and vigilante whose eagle eye had made her Nana feel safe, from a pocket of the humongous winter coat patched and pelted with oblongs of fur. It was hideous, but one that she loved (in part, she thought, *because* it was hideous and had once kept her Nana warm). It kept her warm too in her badly heated Fargo basement flat with its boarded-up windows.

She kept the engine running in the pickup, clumped in cleats to the fish house door and worked the lock loose with fingers that felt frostbit; wet, they might freeze fast to the lock. There was a movie she remembered where a school kid put his tongue on a pole in the cold and got stuck; the image made her laugh. She kicked aside a frozen burbot, a big ugly fish nobody ever kept. Her uncle went for walleyes, always getting more than his limit because nobody bothered much about limits anymore, when she and her Nana had fished with him many moons ago. Good eating, she thought. She had also fished with her boyfriend after their lovemaking, and once she brought up a big flopping thing. "A tullibee," her boyfriend had pronounced with disdain. A Canadian whitefish full of bones. "Too bad it's too big to toss back."

Once inside, she could see that the holes in the ice were half frozen. She started up the propane heater, put it on high, and with a blunt hatchet hacked open one of the fish holes, the largest one, though whether it would be big enough for what she had to do, she refused to think about.

She saw a length of abandoned fishing line wound in a loose coil on the concrete floor. A twisted skein of lies, she thought. She loved the way the phrase echoed, and she said it aloud to hear the vowels and consonants braid together.

Her voice sounded tinny and haunted and echoed in the shack.

She went back out, careful to latch the door from the outside, and sat in the truck for a while. She stared past the shack to the makeshift town on the ice. Three snowmobiles churned up snow and zoomed in a race along the plowed ice roads. A family of four, all big and chunky specimens of the Upper Midwest, full of corn-fed beef, juggled their ice shack off a trailer. They were hard at it, though a young one stopped to pelt the others with snowballs.

Nothing registered. She could imagine the family gathered inside by a propane stove eating ham sandwiches on white bread plastered with mayonnaise and butter. She procrastinated, though she didn't have a watch; the pickup was an older model without an onboard clock. She was unobserved, that was obvious, almost cozy in the cold, safe and free, which was a good thing, because she burst into a frenzy of compulsive activity that might have aroused the suspicions of a bystander.

Inside the shack, where she held the bundle over the largest hole in the ice, she did what she had decided had to be done; but a court of law, a jury, would have been hard put to call it premeditation. With the heel of one shoe, she tried to push the entire bundle through the ice, but something caught and she couldn't manage it. So she shook it, nearly hysterical now, and her companion finally came free and floated under the bundle of blanket. She reached for a rusted shovel and used its sharp blade to hack down while she uttered a sound like a seal or like any animal that might live year-round unconscious under the ice, until perhaps one winter day the right fisherman might bring it up—some strange hybrid specimen that at first glance would appear to be different from anything he had ever seen. A big prune. A giant pickle.

He would be using a three-pronged hook and the Swedish Pimple for bait that her boyfriend had sworn by. He had told her, more than once, for it was his mantra, that the two of them, together forever, might catch something amazing, something never seen before, if they stayed faithful to the Swedish Pimple. To seal the deal, he had given her a gift, a plastic monkey the size of a grape from a gumball machine.

She had always believed him, but now understood it was just something he said—that he would say to someone else with the same

I've-never-said-this-to-anyone conviction that had made her feel so unique. It was just something to say, she thought. Everything is just something to say.

Still, she said a few words. Nothing in particular. Nobody who heard it could call it praying. She had wept and gnashed her teeth when the life had ebbed. There had been nothing to do. Nowhere to go. There was no medicine anymore for somebody without the money to pay. And medicine would have done no good, she thought. Whatever was wrong had been too broken to fix. She had the baby, alone; would never have allowed it to grow like a cancer inside her if she hadn't been too frightened that she might be charged with murder. It came out without a whimper. It came out stone-cold dead.

Gone to a better place, she thought, and laughed at the absurdity.

She knew that she would be home by dark, cozy more or less under covers. She wondered if the place would still feel like home. It was safe where she was, with boarded-up windows, loaded gun, with an acquaintance nearby, though he was as old as Nana had been when death took her. A group of people she knew—she couldn't really call them friends—were ginning up a convoy to make its way to Tulsa.

Tulsa had been Nana's magic word to conjure up justice and paradise. But her Nana had trusted the open road. She had grown up miserable, sometimes beaten, first by her migrant father and then her husband, who had done something terrible to Ava that nobody talked about. And they could never get out of debt. Nobody ever did anymore.

Tulsa. She was thinking about it as she gathered up the empty bundle of blankets, locked the fish house, and decided. It was time to get the hell out of the Dakotas, face the future. Get up and go. Nothing anymore to stay for.

The Girl on the Beach

Ava couldn't help it. She was drawn to certain men who lived in bleak, lonely habitats. When she was lucky, and it was luck, nothing but, they were good to her. Straight now, holding to sobriety like a life raft, she fantasized about a life with Serena, the daughter she had lost, had given away really, let's be honest, in the time when the next fix was her only ambition. She had returned to Fargo, searched without luck, but couldn't let go of hope, however slight, and had fallen in with McGaw—what a name, only McGaw, nothing else—who was kind and took her with him to his small, ruined house on the rocky shore of a great lake where the rough water spoke in a language she understood. She had been someplace like it more than once in the past.

McGaw thought he saw Serena, whose childhood photograph adorned the wall over their bed, balancing on the rocks in the surf. "But really," Ava said, waking beside him. She touched his hand. "No, don't switch on the light." She preferred to listen in the dark. And she was tired, bone-tired. There was something in him that wouldn't let her sleep, some force worming into her until she woke. "You satisfied?" she asked. "Now that I'm up? Is that what you wanted?" Insomnia seldom left her alone.

She was glowing like abalone, McGaw explained, visible in moonlight, her dress fluttering in the lake wind, cries audible. "She was calling out to you. Can't you see?" he said. "It would prove everything. It would show something exciting is going on. Which I know there is; but knowing is one thing, actually seeing's another."

She rubbed her eyes. She had met McGaw at a lamplit séance. He was familiar with Ouija boards and tarot cards and occult lore. He knew about invisible worlds and the dark web. He shuffled pseudonyms the way others work a pack of playing cards. He assuaged her grief over a life lost. Mother. Daughter. Heroin. The three loves of her life, all gone.

She had quit her job without notice to be with him.

She had taken up painting in Fargo, had studied with a self-proclaimed genius, lost herself in paint when she felt the need for a fix. She had faith in art; she would find the right rhythm, the right form. Complete the painting. One painting. It would be her life's work. It would speak, urgently, to any man or woman who stood before it with due diligence.

Their secluded beach house had a wood-burning stove and a tiny artist's studio. Nobody bothered them. She stood, her joints aching, before the canvas each day as the light changed. She could only stare, eyes burning, at what she had wrought, couldn't bring herself to work in the luminous fast-drying tones of egg tempura, an old Renaissance technique she had struggled to master. It was a new life. She knew nothing about painting but stood there day after day. She had once lived in such solitude with a painter, a man who had turned her into a slave. McGaw didn't care. She had no idea what he did when he wandered alone into the woods or along the rowdy shore. The more she waited on the half-finished canvas, brush in hand, attempting to obliterate her personality for the sake of art and sobriety, the more restless McGaw became.

She knew her situation was all wrong, the inverse of that relationship years ago when her lover, the painter, kept her fixed up and compliant in a place just as isolated as this one, only more so. And now there would be another hour, or two, or more, until dawn. He would prowl the dark outside. "Maybe it's nothing," he said, "but maybe this is what we've been waiting for." He continued nagging, so she turned on the lamp and pulled herself from bed, every bone in protest. In the narrow hallway, on the small back porch, chill rushed through her gown. "I need a witness," he said. "You should come. You're a part of this."

"I'm here, aren't I?"

They stared across the sandy yard, coated with dew, to the cave-like shadows of the studio. A shack, really. There was a glimmer, a brief splash of light, elusive. A metallic odor, like blood, filled the air around her. It gave her a start, but it was a tatter of bright cloth, polyester maybe, an old skirt flapping like a bird, caught in screen mesh. She would admit that much. But the door was latched. Who would climb through the windows of a desolate shack? Certainly not her grown daughter. Only him, plagued by delusions. Only he would imagine a tattered skirt draped around the pale waist of a girl he had never met. And who the hell was he to assume her daughter was a spirit, dead to the world except in visions?

He slipped on his khakis. She knew it was useless to plead. He smelled of mildew and metal. He strapped a camera over a shoulder. He took in her bright stare. "You coming?"

An antagonism flared, an anger. It would be nervous doodles in her sketchpad until dawn, the desire for dope flaring up with exhaustion. There was at least that—no dope out here to tempt her.

"She's there," he repeated. "Your daughter. Serena. If you watch, you'll see that flicker like a candle. She's not coming back forever.

She doesn't know she's gone. She thinks she's lost. She left the world too fast. She's in shock." He tottered down the back steps as though plagued with rheumatism. He looked tubercular making his way across the yard, even the baggy khakis unable to disguise his pipe-stem legs, even heavy flannel failing to protect his concave chest.

The chill overcame her. The stiff leather of the hunting jacket worked like sandpaper. Against her will she shook with fright. She had wanted solitude, not pathological isolation. Every cracked-off slat or stain was evidence. Or so you would think, listening to him. Besides, she thought again, anger flaring, who was he to her to claim her daughter was dead?

Exhaustion took him down near dawn. She stood in the studio before the canvas. Century postcards, wooden packing crates, old books with pages stuck together. Dregs. Often now, he spoke of nothing but Serena. It was obscene. Her winsomeness, white skin, long nails. "She's our point of access. She was abducted, brought here by a crazed carpenter, bludgeoned to death in her sleep."

Skag would be better than this, Ava thought.

She wrapped herself in a woolen robe and switched off the lamp, ignoring wooden crates, makeshift bookshelves. There was a faint smell of skunk. The spirit of the place was dissolute, dampness seeping into pores, soaking nerve endings. In the dark she admitted failure. The move, the commitment to McGaw, the painting. What had she been thinking? It was crazy. Her life was finished. Her people dead.

What she had left: one day at a time. One fucking day at a time. Bill is my one friend in the world.

"We're soulmates," McGaw had said to her once, briquettes sputtering in the grill on one of those perfect evenings in Fargo, with sun easing and clouds like mountains in the big sky. In his beret, a scarf around his neck, he was heroic, handsome like the doomed and mythical Kurt Cobain, ravaged face emerging from shadow, and she had taken his words to heart.

He was her type. It was fate.

When she woke, McGaw was gone. She warmed herself with coffee then went searching: bird sanctuary, hiking trails, deserted marina.

Once, in Fargo, he had disappeared for three days.

"How dare you!" she shouted when he returned, unshaven, dissipated.

He smiled and shrugged, an apology. "Three days," he said, waving an arm in dismissal. "Looking at myself like a sculpture, examining life from every side, then eliminating what doesn't belong. Now I can give myself to you. I did it for you. I love you. Let's go away, forget everything."

"Go? Where?"

"I have a place."

She stopped searching a mile from the lake house, the sky dark like milky, black tea. Great clouds wheeled into sight as if announcing yet another plague. How many could there be? She pulled her shawl close.

Something moved.

She turned. Nothing.

Only a lonely loon, rasp of wind, gray light, stunted black oaks tenaciously holding their own, dim green forms of gaunt pines. She sat with her head against a tree.

"This kind of loneliness draws her like a magnet," he had said. "Mirrors her soul. Coincidence. Synchronicity. I feel it. If we take what we see and re-create it, she'll come."

It was insanity.

Someone screamed her name. Or was it rough water, nerves? She could see him floating face down. A wolf finished him, left a torso, slivers of bone. The sheriff pulled up to the house, lowered his head in respect. He brought her to the morgue, a small gray room.

But it wasn't the morgue. It was dark, muddy; she couldn't breathe. The sheriff approached, waving pork-fat arms.

She shook awake, pulled on sandals.

Two days later, he was still missing.

They came quickly when she called, the sheriff and his deputy. One took notes. "We'll put it on the radio." The sheriff nodded. "An APB." They took off hats and scratched heads in unison. It almost made her laugh. "We'll let the Militias know. They have people everywhere."

Overcome by their bulk, blank stares, close to hysteria, she breathed from the diaphragm to maintain self-control. The big one, the sheriff, squinted through the windows of the studio, kicked open the latched door, gun drawn.

She heard him laugh. Was he looking at her painting?

The deputy stared at her. His puffy eyes reminded her of those on a goldfish she had once swallowed in a drinking bout. "Any strangers?"

"No. Why?"

"No reason. Just checking. There've been incidents. Some serious." He squinted. "There's a lot of craziness hereabouts."

"Is there something else?" she asked. "What incidents?"

He puckered his lips and shook his head. "Just checking." He moved, a thought occurring. "What kind of firearm do you keep handy?"

The sheriff came out of the shack. "It's not a place a man in his right mind would want to be. At least not by himself. But there's an old mattress in there, been used not so long ago." He held up a limp condom. "Your husband know anybody but you?"

She turned away.

"No offence. Just checking. You the painter? Or is he the culprit?"

She narrowed her eyes.

He grinned. "We remember your husband. He was stationed up here, when there used to be somewhere up here to get stationed. He had a few friends. Some of those people who live in the woods and only come out at night. They have more power now hereabouts than they did then."

They stood by the squad car, talking in low voices, smirking, sharing a joke, the sheriff's hard, creased face icy with gallows humor. The deputy pointed to her, one index finger cocked like a gun. The sheriff tipped his hat and hitched up his pants. "We'll check on you now," he called across the yard. "You're a ways from people. You let us know if he shows up."

She didn't know what to do, where to look. Once they left, she stood in the windswept yard, near a small patch of garden where something was trying to grow. She walked over to the stalk and tugged.

She couldn't drive: The broken car, covered with its plastic tarp, was parked near the house, looming like a prehistoric worship stone.

"It's all a fraud," she said, startling herself. She would leave the painting where it was. That part of her life was over. Even the passionate rhythms of sex, insatiable physical desire, had grown oppressive. Out here, McGaw had turned into something she wanted to push away quick.

"Goodbye then," she said aloud. She packed a bag. Sadness overwhelmed her. She would find her way back to Fargo and start from square one. Or head for Tulsa. Or the Southwest, where she knew a guy who could get her work, if she arranged for an unblemished ID, as a border guard. She was at the kitchen table, writing McGaw a note, when he rushed into the house.

"I was after her. I found her!" His eyes were bright, feverish. "She spoke to me. She had a lot to say!" He staggered about the room, limping, favoring his right ankle. "Something happened to my ankle. I didn't bruise it, it didn't get twisted, it just started hurting!"

She clutched the end of the table, its cold metal fluting.

"She was that close," he said, holding his hands a foot apart. "Then she disappeared. Let's use that old sailboat down the beach." He tore at a loaf of bread, a block of cheese. "You know that glow? It's not a candle, a flashlight. It's some kind of bacteria, like Day-Glo paint. Under her skin!" He gulped down milk. "I came to get you. I need help."

"No. I'm going back."

"Going back?" He folded his arms. A primitive mask of rage engraved itself on his features. It brought to mind the man who'd beat her. The one she'd killed. "You're staying. If you're not here when I get back, I swear I'll find you." He tilted against the door. "I could kill you, you know that?"

She felt her fists clench. "Yeah? You and who else?" She felt tears come.

"Your marvelous genius," he said. "Why don't we go pay your genius a visit?"

"You must be crazy," she said. She forced her fingers to relax. "You must be out of your mind. What's wrong with you? Are you using?"

"Oh, come off it," he said, waving a hand in dismissal. He smiled. Ingratiating. "It's just a way of talking. Anyway, I've heard you say it—that time in Fargo they had the music so loud? 'I wish I had a gun,' you said. 'I'd blow their heads off.'"

"That was nothing like what you just did." Her head felt foggy.

"Come here," he said. He motioned to her, using a gesture she always associated with intimacy. "Let's make up." He motioned again, the gesture even more intimate. "Ava, your daughter; she's a succubus. I need you there. We've got to hurry to the boat. We can save her. You can see her again."

"No." She chose her words carefully. "I'll wait here. I won't go anywhere."

He stared at her, hard, then walked away. The women, she thought. It's always a woman, alone with the men, when they go off their rockers. She waited a few minutes, breathing herself down, repeating a mantra, a form of the serenity prayer.

She took to the road with her duffel bag. After a few miles of chill in the woods, the road turned back close to the lake and a lonesome café. With its exposed siding and faded sign cracked down the middle, it served as a bus depot. The locals—unemployed lumberjacks, miners, Militia members—gathered to drink coffee. Two weathered faces stared through the plate-glass window, filmy with dust.

A bus was due. She waited outside in her black hoodie. The air was heavy; clouds gathered over the lake. Across the road the sheriff stood by his patrol car, his arms folded. He tipped his hat. A car taxied past, the driver rubbernecking her, but finally the gray bulk of the bus edged into the shell-covered lot. The driver, gaunt, fossil-like, opened the door. She hesitated, then climbed into an odor of ash and perspiration. She pulled a face mask from the pocket of her hoodie and put it on, just to be safe.

The sheriff caught her eyes before the bus rattled south. She turned from the tinted window, from his icy smile and the lake behind him. Before she did, she noticed a sailboat on the lake with a lantern swinging from its bow in the dusk. It was far out, almost at the horizon, heading for open water.

The Hummingbird

Mika's husband, cop gofer by day and wannabe Marauder by night, had long ago convinced her that her Indian blood was something to live down, not celebrate, and now she accepted that the locked room adjacent to the kitchen where he kept his sacred totem (his phrase) was taboo. She understood that she had disappointed him, that she was no longer the woman he had married, the woman who had crooned songs from her childhood as she kept the house clean. Even so, she could not finger the crime that had convinced him to take each card in turn—the credit card, the department store card, the gasoline card—and snip it into a dozen pieces, clench a fist full of plastic, and toss the bits into the bin.

"There!" he said, glaring.

"You spend more than I do," she said, breath difficult to locate, as though he had punched her in the belly. In fact, it had been more than a week since he'd beat her, which had to be a good thing, but her head turned dizzy and she wondered if she might be having a stroke. Things between them had not been so bad this week, but the contents of her purse, strewn over the kitchen table; the metal clasps of her coin purse, poking a hole in the plastic wrapper of a loaf of bread; her checkbook, flung open on the dull linoleum floor; and a tampon in the butter dish all told a different story.

"What have you done?" she asked. She bent down to pick up the checkbook, but he stepped in front of her and slipped it into a back pocket of his camouflage pants.

"We will not spend money," he said. "We must scrimp. I've been assigned a mission." He took the green lampshade off the kitchen lamp and the unshielded bulb forced her to squint. He sat her down to interrogate. "We will pay off debt. We will not keep money in banks. We will buy gold and silver. When there is no money, we will do without. Your daughter will not be spoiled."

Lillooet, her wild onion, was not his. Though Mika had not heard from her daughter's birth father since back in the day, she knew enough about mood to keep her mouth shut. "I'm putting you on strict notice," her husband said. "This checkbook will go to my name and mine alone. You must account for every goddamned penny, either now or in your next life. We are warriors and must live as such."

The word "warrior," coming from him, made her stomach lurch. Afraid that his voice would waken Lillooet, she closed the door that separated the kitchen from the rest of the rented house. "You might be right," she said carefully. "I have not been careful enough." She smelled urine. Or something. On his breath, maybe, some kind of booze.

In fact, she had squirreled away a thousand dollars in cash, most of it a gift from her sister—"getaway money"—some scrimped and saved over the past year. She did it the way she kept a hummingbird inside her head, an invisible spiderweb charm, to guide her when she felt lost. She called it deep-brain massage.

Satisfied, he poured coffee, put the shade back on the lamp, and motioned as though actually helping her clean the mess. She knew that's how he would remember it, as assistance. Once he completed his rant, and it took some time, he retreated to the room where he spent so much of his life. She sat at the zinc table and heard him mutter, heard him open and close books and preach to an invisible congregation. All the crazy things people believed had made him crazy, and she had to repeat it all when she was with him and pretend she too believed it, crazy talk.

If she went to the tribe, where she had never really been, that might be her name: Walking-on-Eggs Mika. It was what some had called her in jest. Lillooet, who had her dark hair and high cheekbones, would be Wild Onion, would experience the lodges and ceremonies, taste the sun as it rose from the plains, move like a flower for four days at the midsummer sun dance. Not like her family, she thought, and saw her father, dressed in a felt hat, a stained duffel coat, and a pair of gray cuffed pants as he spoke with a medicine man whose eyes radiated a glow like obsidian, who wore leggings and moccasins, feathers and fringe, a beautiful choker necklace of beads and turquoise. "We live and then we live again," the medicine man said. "If you come clean, the door is there and you are made welcome." The fierce man leaned close to her mild father. She had been hypnotized by the turquoise stone staring like an eye from the hollow of his chest. He had a magical pouch slung around one wrist. "Ascend the red road. Walk in the sacred manner," he finished. It was a common phrase.

Her father, unimpressed, had taken off his felt hat, scratched his head, stared into the overcast sky darkened by high buildings, and changed the subject. "That guy's a clown," he told her afterward, "making it up as he goes along. Don't be impressed by bullshit." He had a job in the city that put food on the table and kept a roof over their heads and was a proud man who worshipped, when he worshipped at all, at a Christian church. "Two of your uncles stayed on the reservation," he told her. "One, you know who I'm talking about, got into liquor and the dope and couldn't stop. He passed. The other one, he's okay; traps leeches, collects cones, harvests wild rice, makes do. He stands proud, has freedom. Mumbo jumbo don't impress him."

Wasn't that how it happened? It was all she had from the old days. She couldn't remember if it had happened that way or if she had made it up herself over time, like a fairy tale, to give her something to hold on to. He had been a good man; she knew that much.

She had told her husband the story once, in the good days, or the better days anyway, and he had come to her during the night, nude and erect, singing. "The medicine man / The medicine man / The medicine man is here," he sang. "And he's got something nice / For you." It had made her laugh. Back then, he was different; they had some good times. Though even back then, she remembered, he liked his sex rough.

The night he cut up her cards and seized her checkbook, she dreamed of the hummingbird, her version of the spiderweb charm, darting near the house. In her dream she was the sleepwalker, and the hummingbird gave her a pouch with medicine and made her understand that it was all she needed.

The next morning, she made him his breakfast and got him off to work with the cops. He had not slept; he was exhausted, eyes red-rimmed, stubble on his cheeks, skin sagging. An old man, she thought. "Pick up the phone each time I call," he said.

He called her maybe a dozen times a day.

She made breakfast for Lillooet and got her off to school. The girl was subdued and groggy, as though medicated. She too lived in a dream, one that could be broken, Mika thought. The house to herself, she spent an hour jiggling through a box of keys, keeping the hummingbird with her, before she found the one that fit the locked door. The room smelled like sweat and whiskey and old newsprint, and she felt an overwhelming urge to fall to the unswept floor and weep. Instead, she forced open a window to air out the room. I'll just clean up the damn place, she thought, but sunlight streamed to his cluttered desk and she sensed that she was breaking their bond. Like the hummingbird, she thought. He liked to tell strangers that he was a technical specialist with the cops; it sounded like big stuff, but in fact he was a clerk. He filled equipment and supply requests, though he did have a license to carry a gun and once, when they were both drinking, had threatened her with it, had made her put its barrel in her mouth. "Sweet, eh?" he asked, perspiration glistening on his forehead. Afterward, contrite, he had wanted her to understand that it was a joke, that the gun was empty.

"The truth is," she had replied impulsively, "you're a lowlife."

He used the word often with his buddies who came to the house to drink and play poker. "Not even good enough to be a cop," she had said. He had beat her, a bad beating, and she had left him, taken Lillooet to her sister's cramped apartment above a greasy dive. Her sister insisted on photographs, but not even threats could make her turn him in to the cops. If she did, they would come and get her, not him. "A man could hunt a woman, beat one, kill one. Don't matter," she told her sister, "unless the lowlife is one they don't like. The cops would get me, not him."

Her sister had pursed her lips thoughtfully. "Then how about make them not like the bastard?"

He had apologized for what he did, even come to her sister's apartment with a bouquet. A bundle of flowers for the first time in her life. "I'll take the cure if you want," he said; "you can scourge my flesh if that's what it takes."

She had returned, but he did not keep his word. Sometimes he whacked her. But not often. Still, she remembered in her loins the passion that had once existed between them. Her eyes found his, her heart jumped, and her blood took him in like a child and lover both.

I'm stupid, she thought. Stuck. The hummingbird goes up and down and back, never stuck, on the move, like the soul. Her mother had put family above freedom, above loyalty. And Lillooet needed a father, didn't she, someone who made a living? At least he had a living.

And now her sister had moved out west close to the ocean. "Call me when you leave him," she told Mika. "In the meantime, keep yourself to yourself."

The gun lay on the desk next to a notebook. Beneath the odor of sweat and whiskey, the room smelled of gun oil. She forgot about the pouch of hummingbird medicine in her head and found the bottle, half empty, behind the desk, next to a moldy magazine of women doing things she could hardly imagine. She took a few tokes. It went down good. She held the bottle to her nose and enjoyed its sharp oak odor, then put it back and tidied up the small paper-cluttered room and sat in his chair in the light to read the notebook.

He sets me in the Center of the Plain filled with Bones. I pay off Debt and walk among the Bones. They come to life with a rattle, Bone joins Bone. The Graves open and the Bones rise and walk. The Beast is disguised as a Man of God. He is Colored, a Spic, a Dago, Jewboy, Queer. A Terrorist. WE will rain down Bullets and Bombs, drown the Shitbrains and Scumbags in their Own Blood. We will cut off Diseased Dicks and stuff them in Bags. They will Drink their Own Blood filthy with AIDS and virus. We will keep Our God Emperor in Power.

It went on like that. The phone rang; she ignored it. She was fascinated. He had bullshit for religion. Bullshit for politics. She should have realized it long ago, when he and his kind frothed at the mouth when their election candidate lost, but there's a first time for everything.

124

He wrote the way she did when she was in third grade or sloppy drunk. She had seen him worship the cops who carried guns, but I mean to tell you, she thought, imitating him, momentarily amused, this shit is flat-out weird. She laughed, momentarily freed from his oppression. The phone rang again, kept ringing, and stopped. That meant he was on his way home in a hurry if he could get away; it wouldn't be the first time, and that was too bad, but she would be damned if she would listen to his gravel-shit voice and let him beat her.

She sat at his desk in a plank of sunlight. How had this happened? She had a cataract in one eye, varicose veins in one leg. Lillooet's life should grow like a plant, she thought, slow, with drums and chants, or just a life of peace and quiet in the city, but what she loved, except for Lillooet, was dead. She picked up the gun. Heavy, like a paperweight. The metal barrel greasy to the touch, rubber grips sticky, coated with his skunk stink. He played with it sometimes, twirled it with a finger in the trigger guard the way a kid plays bandito.

She cradled it.

I could blow his fucking head off.

Or blow my own goddamned head off.

Sunlight flooded the room; dust motes hung suspended. She reached to the desk and closed the book. She couldn't stand his handwriting because it was his hand, writing—a cramped, crooked scrawl of poison. Like the gun. She dropped the gun on top of the book as if both objects were sticky with his stink.

She hated every bastard who had put her where she was.

She became drunk with hate.

"We live again," the medicine man had told her father. "We live and then we live again." It was the same thing, more or less, that the Christian minister would say.

Or was she making it up? The years take so much from us.

"To go on a quest is good," the medicine man said. He stared at her. "It's good to be in transit." She turned quickly, but the room was

125

empty, the door shut tight. A room of shit, she thought, filled with the noise of the stupid. Medicine man, my ass. My father was right. Fucking men. All the same. Worship ME; that's what they all say.

She sat very still, rubbed away goose bumps, and worked the thing out. The pouch, she thought. That's my object. That's my thing. Then she picked up the gun and put it between her belt and flesh; she took his book into the yard, lit a match, and burned its pages. They crinkled and blackened to ash. The breeze took bits and blew them over the collapsing chain-link fence.

When her father was dying, he had raved about a potlatch, a burning ceremony where everything that could not be sent to paradise with the corpse, or given away, went up in flames. It was ancient history, nothing Ojibwa or Christian, but a thing he wanted. Burn it up, start over. So she had burned his felt hat and his overcoat, stood and stared into the sky as stars took notice of the flames. His forehead and limbs were themselves on fire with fever, heat radiating from every wrinkled pore, and the last thing she did after the busk was bathe him with a wet cloth.

I was a hummingbird then, she thought. I flew. I had hummingbird medicine.

She had once been a drunk, and her husband was still a drunk. It had taken her this long to get over her dry drunk. Confronting him would make for drama, and her life had been too long without drama, the right kind of drama. But he was drunk not just on whiskey but on the Bible and junk he heard and believed. That was the worst kind of drunk. People drunk on the word of God, convinced of their righteousness, would do anything to anybody. And he was hungover from whiskey. A smoky shape flitted in the corner of her bad eye with the cataract.

She put the thousand dollars in her purse and called Lillooet's school. This is my potlatch, she thought. It's time. She knew that there would be a price to pay for years of slavery to a bad man, but the price would be less if she paid it sooner, so she closed the suitcase and lugged it to the back door, which slammed behind her. She heard his truck screech around the corner and fishtail to a stop at the curb. She dragged the grip—her father had called it such—across the yard behind some bushes and a wooden fence on its last legs. In untucked flannel and old jeans, she waited, bent knees aching. She could smell fresh-turned soil and see a rusty red wheelbarrow half hidden by trash. She could feel the gun against her midriff.

He didn't stay long, only glanced out back, shouted her name twice, and then screeched off in his truck. She stayed crouched where she was, working out something in her head, then went into the house and did what she had to do before she left for good. She put the gun back where she had found it. She would take nothing that belonged to him.

At the school a few minutes later, she picked up Lillooet, who frowned and bit a thumbnail. "Anything in your locker you can't do without?" Lillooet shook her head. "Then let's go, you and me. A long way." Mika took her hand. "I have a hummingbird with me in a pouch. A secret pouch. Want to see?"

Lillooet said nothing. She scowled, perhaps thinking of the journey ahead.

"This road is a good road, a good road," Mika said, and then decided it was a stupid thing to say—a false thing to keep courage up—and she became nervous, glancing over a shoulder.

Already the house belonged just to him, and to the past. He was the true enemy of the Antichrist, he had told her, beating it into her head like a drum, and she had given him credit for powers barely human.

He would burn rubber to the school, and his work shoes would thump as he ran to the office. She had left the gun and hoped he would carry it into school. Something bad will happen, she thought, and that's good. Something bad enough to read about in the papers. They won't like him anymore. The bastard.

Then she remembered the hummingbird in her pocket and let him go.

Once she boarded the bus with her pouch and her grip and Lillooet, she paid the fare. Maybe he would kill somebody or shoot himself. If I had stayed, I would have shot him, she thought. With his own gun.

No middle ground.

She sat on the long seat in the back of the bus next to a woman in a black hoodie wearing a mask. The woman reached into one of the hoodie's pockets and held out more masks. "I have extra," she said. "You and your girl should put them on."

Mika took them and chucked her head in thanks, too shy to speak.

The woman in the hoodie tilted her head and pointed down the aisle. "You see?" she said, croaking the words in a scratchy voice. "All women aboard. Even the driver. You see? When men go off their rockers, we women all have to hightail it. And here we are." She made a slight, creaking sound that might have been a laugh. "Look me in the eyes," she said. "I can tell you're also on the run."

Mika did as requested and stared into the madwoman's bright eyes. She smelled stale perfume and diesel fumes and felt dizzy. The woman's eyes went deep. "If a man puts you in the cross, remember my eyes and ask me what to do. I will tell you, and you will hear what I say. And then what?"

"Huh?"

"And then, honey, you do it. Just do it. Used to be a slogan back in the day, remember? Just do it! Don't take any guff from the swine." She nodded as if admiring her own advice. "I'm Ava, honey. And you are?"

"Mika."

"Beautiful name. And your little girl?"

"Lillooet," Mika said, and added, shyly, "Wild Onion."

"Beautiful name. Beautiful girl." Ava nodded and kept nodding, as if she was a doll with a spring in her neck. "I like that. Remember what I said." She stopped wagging her head and stared hard again. "You remember, yes?"

"Just do it," Mika said, afraid to say anything else.

Ava continued staring until Mika turned away. She would never forget the look in the woman's eyes.

Twice along the route the bus stopped and armed Militia entered and studied the faces of passengers, comparing them to photos on their phones. A heavyset man in a mask that was dark black and covered almost all of his face, like a balaclava, came to the back of the bus and motioned to Mika to lower her mask. She did so and stared at him, hard, thinking what Ava had said. Ava was doing the same and still had on her hoodie, which Mika thought took nerve. The Militia man ignored Ava but studied Mika as if she was a math problem. Finally he put his phone in a pocket and turned without a word. Mika watched him stomp down the aisle, thinking that he waddled like a putz. She put her mask back on.

When the bus later lurched to a stop, the end of the line, Mike offered to return the masks. Ava shooed her away. "Keep them," she said. "Use them again." She gave Mika a sign with one clenched hand. "And remember what I said."

Mika took Lillooet by the hand. Outside the bus, they started walking, climbing a steep hill as her heart tattooed her ribs. They walked past swaybacked houses on the wrong side of town and she knew he was cruising the city, the gun on the seat beside him, but nobody bothered her and his green truck stayed lost.

"Let me see the hummingbird," Lillooet said.

"It's not the kind I can show you," she said. When you give up being a slave, life becomes possible. Who had told her that? Her sister? "But we're going to see Auntie, girl, and she has a hummingbird just like mine."

She had given up smoking when she was pregnant; had given up drinking, most of the time, after he beat her nearly to death; and now, without a fight, she was giving him up, he who had always put a roof over their heads and food on the table, and had beaten her badly only a few times. Just now and then. Well, maybe there were other times, she realized, ones she might remember one day. He wasn't that bad, was he? Maybe she should go back.

She bought a bag of burgers and rented a cheap room in a motel under a name that was not hers. The room was dumpy, and Lillooet frowned again. "I want to see your hummingbird!"

"Stomp your foot, why don't you?" Mika teased. "But let's eat first, okay?" A lot of talking would have to pass between them, but this was not the time. She could see neon blink through dirty gauze curtains on the room's barred window. She heard the clank of a train on its tracks, a big truck switch gears, somebody close shout out swear words. None of it bothered Lillooet, done to a turn; she was soon asleep mumbling in her clothes, lying on the thin bedspread with the half-eaten burger beside her.

Mika, ravenous, finished it off and then devoured the last one with its thin disc of greasy meat. If that's meat, she thought, stifling a laugh, I'm the queen of Sheba.

Anyway, the two of them had gone far enough for the day. Each day is a journey and begins with one step. Each long journey ends with a curse, like a man with a gun or a minister with a Bible standing over a gravestone and saying something so wrong that nobody near him can argue with it.

But there are drums and chants in the world too, music and sisters with room to spare, not just bad men with guns and Bibles and stupid thoughts. There was a ladder in her chest to climb, something besides regret to remember. And they were further west than they had been that morning, closer to the faraway ocean and to her sister, who would welcome them with open arms. She promised herself for Lillooet's sake, and her own, that this would be an adventure, no trail of tears.

She clutched her pouch in one clenched hand, afraid to open it because the hummingbird might fly free. And laughed. There was no pouch to clutch, but there it was, in her hand. "Hummingbird Mika," she said, and heard her voice echo in the sparse room filled with the soggy spirits of others.

She said it a second time for good measure. "Hummingbird Mika."

No more Walking-On-Eggs.

Border Guards

"People are, like, heading north? You notice that?" Ava said.

He had just arrived. His uniform was crisp, but his dark skin already glistened with sweat even inside the guard station.

Ava stared with dull eyes. "Dude," she said, "another drink." She held out her empty glass.

"You angry at what I did last night?" he said. He poured her more vodka.

She tried to remember what he had done. Was he confusing her with some other *puta*? She put the tumbler on the table in front of her without taking a swig. "People are nice up north. Most of them, anyway. It's cold sometimes. We stay safe in the cold."

"Never been," he said. "Down here? On the border? I feel safe. Keep out the ones who don't belong." The two were inside a small Butler building, predesigned with Thermawall panels and a standing-seam metal roof system. Secure. Sensors everywhere. An old air-conditioning unit did its best to keep the place tolerable. Ava's khaki uniform needed a wash real bad. Her companion, young but bald-headed, maybe with his scalp shaven, had a broken front tooth. What was the story with that? He had only arrived yesterday, so his uniform was still starchy. He looked to Ava like a gap-toothed, dark-skinned clown. All he needed was face paint and lipstick. She laughed.

He scowled. "You shoot anybody?" he said. "You kill anyone?" Her two weeks were done. He was there to replace her. That's what border security came to in this part of the desert. There was no wall. No water, either, for that matter—just the dry river wash, chicken wire, and sensors. Safer here than anyplace else, probably.

She startled, contemplated the glass of clear liquid. "You mean ever?"

He laughed unpleasantly. "No, I mean now. Here and now. In the past two weeks. Anybody try to cross? Anybody try to pay you off?" He grinned. "Or fuck you?"

"Does knifing a guy in the back count?"

It was his turn to startle. "You knifed a guy?"

"God, no," she said. "I'm just thinking aloud. Your back looks in need of a knife."

"You're a beaner, aren't you?" he said. He was rubbing his hands together, looking her over. "You like it rough, don't you?"

"I'm a beaner the way you're a drug dealer, dude. And I'm sure you've heard worse. The N-word, for example? Calling somebody a beaner tells me all I need to know about you. You don't know a damn thing about who I am or where I come from."

"The N-word?" he said. "You're thinking it, aren't you?"

"No, dude, not thinking it, not saying it. I can honestly tell you that not once in my awful, tainted life—not one single, damned time—have I spoken that word or thought it to myself. The men I've known with dark skin who've treated me like shit? I throw the same words at them I throw at anybody else who does me wrong."

134

"Yeah? Like what?"

"Asshole. Jerk off. Piece of shit. Misogynist. Good-for-nothing. That enough?"

"You started it," he said, staring down now, biting his bottom lip.

"Nyah, nyah, nyah. You kidding me, right?" She was calm now, collected, or maybe dazed after two weeks alone in the desert keeping a logbook, checking out the beeps that indicated trespass, living alone with her thoughts. "Actually, I'm a mama; that's what I am. Call me that if you call my anything."

He took it in as though it was a piece of buttered toast. "I apologize," he said. "I truly am. I don't know why I said that. Maybe because you have so much sympathy for them. The beaners." She laughed in disbelief, hearing him repeat the word, but he looked like he meant it, the apology, with his mouth open so that she could see between his discolored teeth. He arched his brows to indicate sincerity. He sat across from her and poured a second drink. "Boy or girl?"

"Girl. Serena. Haven't seen her in a very, very long time." She bit her tongue. The last thing she would do in front of this guy was break down in weepy weakness.

He stared, maybe feeling for her and thinking that he had two weeks to work himself into the condition she was in. "That's too bad. Beautiful name. She up north?"

"Don't know," she said. "I gave her a phone. Don't know why I can't bring myself to call the number. Maybe I'm hoping, you know, that it's still hers? And know that it isn't? As ridiculous as that sounds. That number has to be long dead. That's for damn sure."

She heard what she had just said. "That doesn't make any sense, does it?" She didn't know why she was telling him stuff. It's what isolation did, made her indifferent to a slapstick clown's opinion. Actually, she thought, he's good-looking, except for that gap between the teeth. She saw her daughter many years ago sitting on a linoleum floor building a mountain from Lego blocks and climbing it with

135

two fingers. "When I grow up," she had said, laughing with delight, "I'm climbing to the real top of a real mountain."

There was a beep from the monitor. Technically, she was on duty until she left, so he let her walk to the console and study the dials. "From the tower east of us. Could be something," she said. "Might be nothing." She shrugged. "Animals, I guess." He laughed. She turned, quick to take offense since she had meant the word literally, just like she said "coyote" literally and something else to indicate smugglers—she hated the dismissive slang her colleagues used every day; she had a code even when down and out—but grinned instead. They were fellow officers, after all. "Story of our lives, eh?" She did a goose-limbed dance back to her chair to amuse him and get loose for the long drive ahead.

He laughed again. "We're waiting for Godot, *Chiquita*."

"*Chiquita*? I'm bigger than you, asshole," she said, surprised he knew the reference. Samuel Beckett: She had seen the play in another lifetime but still remembered most of it. Her tone deflated them both. She knew he wanted to fuck her, a farewell fuck. They had had a go once or twice, nothing but comfort food. Hello and goodbye, have a nice two weeks. He knew she knew what he was thinking, but he wasn't the type to try anything gonzo. She could tell, though, by the way he filled her tumbler to the rim with vodka, that he wanted to get lucky. "Or just drunk." She said those last three words aloud.

A ticking time bomb. She had spent her life listening to such ticks, waiting for the explosion. "No more," she said. "That vodka?" she said. "You want me to pour it down the sink? Or you want it?"

He startled again. "You driving out tonight? What's the hurry?"

She could read the disappointment as if it was a book for kids. "My body is clean of everything but booze," she said. "I have a daughter. Her name is Serena. I told you that. I'm going to find her, by hook or crook. She might be wondering what's happened to me. If I give a damn. It's a scratch I have to itch." She took a breath. "Or something like that. I've been remiss. For a long time. Too long. It's probably too late. But who knows? If the phone number don't work, I'll get up north and look around. Or check out Tulsa. Last time I was up in Fargo, Tulsa was Mecca. The Land of Milk and Honey. It was like an itch everybody had to scratch. Seemed like lots of people head there sooner or later. Hard to figure, right? Tulsa, of all places." How many nights had she beaten herself to a pulp with guilt? And how many nights had she decided against doing anything at all? I'm not ready, she told herself. Not yet. It was a peculiar taboo.

He considered her words. He nodded. "Only one way to find out, I guess." He moved her drink to his side of the table. "Do it. Don't put it off. We all have regrets."

"Thank you for that," she said. She could tell he thought she was being strong, doing the right thing, and to help her stay strong had risen above his desires. It made him desirable, but she wasn't interested. He was still a clown, though she felt vague affection. She didn't feel strong. Anything but. The odds that the old phone number might reach the daughter abandoned so long ago—under duress, admittedly—weren't good. It was a fantasy. She knew that. It was probably why she couldn't bring herself to dial. One shred of dignity still left in the tank. If the number was kaput, she would feel like a funeral that she had to attend every day for the rest of her life. How could she track down a daughter when she herself had been missing in action for so many years? Did she think her daughter was waiting to hear from her?

The monitor beeped again. He stood, stretched, and walked to the barred window to stare outside as if a prisoner doing time. The air conditioner didn't help much. She could smell her stink. It filled the room. She should have aired out the shack and showered before he arrived. It embarrassed her.

She watched him from where she sat. She could feel a mania coming and fought against it. "North Dakota," she said. "It's a good

137

place to go back to. There're some good people up there. It might not be a place to live a life, but I wouldn't mind returning there when it's my time."

"People nearby," he said, clicking a fingernail against the monitor's screen. "Three, maybe four." He walked to the window.

"You can't see anybody from there, through that window," she said. "If they're there, let them be. Some of the Americans already stateside, some here their entire lives, are filth, but they scream, 'Send them back where they came from.' Can you imagine any decent human being shouting such a thing? Such people are filth. Let the ones outside in. They can't be worse than what we have. It'll be an improvement."

He shook his head. "We have to saddle up," he said. "Who knows? They could be coming after us. Those Marauders and Militias springing up." He holstered himself, reached for his Glock 47, special made for the border, and a rifle. "You coming?" he said.

"No, dude. I'm not. Happy trails."

He stared hard at her.

"It's nothing," she said. "Let it be." She repeated the name "Serena" in her head like a prayer. She had the number memorized. She wouldn't let him distract her.

He stood like a statue, clenching and unclenching his fingers.

"I'm off duty," she said. "Don't go after nobody. Call a drone. If you must."

"I need the job," he said. "They don't just monitor them. They monitor us too. You know that. Things have changed. This ain't a democracy."

She shrugged. "It is, for me. A democracy of one. Stay safe," she said.

He left without goodbye. She heard him fire up the ATV. It backfired, gained traction, and roared into the desert. She decided she would go to North Dakota first, and then, if she had no luck, to Tulsa. Or maybe stop first in Tulsa, which wasn't that far away. The city had been her mother's Holy Grail. "Everything copacetic there, Ava," she had said, daydreaming. "The Police are professional. The housing affordable. The people friendly."

"Oh, yeah?" Ava had said, stoned, cynical. "Sounds like bliss."

She cringed at the memory. The past embarrassed her almost every day. Had there ever been a time when she wasn't stoned-cold exhausted? Or just stoned? And other people's meanness had made her mean. She tried to remember Serena. What she looked like. How it had felt, holding her. Squirmy. A squirmy thing. A smile like no other. She ran her fingers through her own stringy hair. She had not been a good mama, even before the troubles.

What had she done?

What the hell had she done?

What on God's good earth had she done?

Not your fault, she heard her own mama say. *You sick. You need help.*

Not every mama is a saint. Ava could say, with hindsight, that hers should be beatified. On the Mexican Day of the Dead, they should build monuments in her name. Fuck Jesús Malverde. Stupid little prick of a drug dealer. Beat the drums and blow the horns for Mama.

She went to the console and played with the cameras. She admitted: guilty. I should have gone with the clown to see what the sensors picked up. Would he have allowed me to go off like that, by myself? Maybe. Maybe. But she had told him to let them be. Why was it on him to keep the lost ones from a foothold in a place that had nothing to offer anyway? Let them find out for themselves. America, home of the predators and the corrupt, born in genocide and slavery and now returning to those roots. The bad guys prevailed. No more truth, no more justice, no more American way.

We should be going after crooks, she thought, not cooks.

She gathered her things, stuffed her duffel. She grunted at the mess. The Jeep outside had to be returned to the mother ship in town. More a fort than a town, she thought. If she tried to get to North Dakota or Tulsa in it, they would apprehend her and that would be that. Even the tires had sensors. She would have to find a slammer good enough to get her to some destination—Tulsa first, she decided—without a breakdown and sturdy enough to keep going in the cold after she made it home. Or the bus. There was always a bus.

Home. Now there's a word. It sounded very strange. Home.

Where the heart is.

What if you don't have a heart?

She pulled out her phone and used an app to figure that Tulsa was more than eleven hundred miles away. If she found nothing there, it was another eight hundred miles to Fargo. Fargo was also a sanctuary, as far as she could tell. Low crime.

The cold, she remembered. Keeps out the riffraff.

If she couldn't find Serena, though, truth was she had no idea what she could do when she got there except sit tight someplace, sling hash at a diner, do her best to stay clean, and think things through. Stay straight.

It was disheartening. How life slips away. The whole goddamned whirligig.

Goddamn it, she thought, I'm going home. Or someplace, anyway.

She took the phone out of her pocket. It was fully charged. She had kept track of things. Her junkie days were gone, though she was aware that the siren call of opioids would forever be her fate.

Once a junkie, always a junkie, she thought.

But not today.

When the desire came to score, the best place to be was the middle of nowhere. She would be on guard every hour of each day. I'm a friend of Bill, she thought, but I would never marry the guy. Booze is also my friend. The routine of staying clean could also kill. She looked across the table at the glass full of vodka.

Irresistible urges pass.

She sat still until this one did. It became a ghost someplace in the room and left her more exhausted than ever. God, she wanted to sleep.

She hit the dial button. She punched in the number she knew by heart, the one she had never forgotten except maybe on her worst days. And worst years.

She listened to the void, to a signal making its way up north. Or not, she thought. She still had hope. She was almost happy as she listened to the phone ring.

And ring. Until it stopped. "Number out of service," a robot voice said.

It was time to go. She didn't know if it was time to go someplace or just to go, hit the road, go for the sake of going. Life didn't feel like much fun anymore. But it wasn't time for it to end. Just go.

PART FOUR
Tulsa

Build Me a House

Serena couldn't wait to get to Tulsa, to know the place, feel its vibe, walk the downtown neighborhoods where massacres had occurred but would never take place again. She could honor the dead, her own and theirs; explore museums that celebrated Woody Guthrie and Bob Dylan; gyrate at the famous club, Cain's, still in business after all these years, more than a century old but by all reports still going strong. She would stare at the downtown Art Deco architecture while eating the wonderful fried okra a friend told her was the best thing she ever tasted. "Fried okra?" she had replied, bemused.

The old Greenwood neighborhood, where the massacre happened so long ago, was now one of many enclaves downtown, an area with an actual police force populated by men and women of all races who actually protected and served. The city was self-contained, she understood, had groceries and drugstores and a hospital and a school and all the mom-and-pop businesses needed to find work. The Marauders were kept at bay. The Militias respected the boundaries. There was festivity, fantasy, lives well lived. It was paradise compared to Fargo or almost anyplace else.

So she had heard.

That was the myth anyway, one she took to heart. And she decided to believe it, come hell or high water, because it made spiritual sense and gave her the push needed to hit the road. She had given up on finding her mother—Ava, she thought, Ava, the palindrome, same from the back or the front. Now she yearned to find her place and stay in it until her itchy feet calmed down.

She endured the long journey over bad roads still passable but no longer maintained in the back of a van with worn shocks and no windows, reluctantly accepting the lack of a view in return for the cheap ride. The van belonged to Wander, a self-described and bumptious nomad, a round-cheeked woman with thick-lensed black-framed eyeglasses and cloudy eyes who was too old for the dyed black hair and pigtails she wore. The van traveled in a caravan with a dozen other vehicles: trucks and trailers, ancient RVs hobbling along, a sedan or two outfitted with sufficient care to call home. Wander was ancient too, with those cataracts she claimed made it difficult to drive, but she allowed nobody else behind the wheel, even though two others, impulsive exiles like Serena, though younger, sat in front with Wander babbling to one another about boys and trinkets. They were sisters, Wander had said, relatives she was bound by blood to help. "Nobody knows the roads or how to drive 'em like me," she said, "but the potholes are murder, aren't they? Upkeep ain't what it used to be."

Serena half listened, sometimes dozing, through a small open rectangle with a sliding plastic window in the steel partition that separated cabin from living quarters. Two old people, probably in their eighties, who told Serena they were called Man and Woman, were dressed in multiple layers of clothing even when the caravan left the upper Midwest and temperatures climbed. They slept and snored beside her on a narrow mattress and woke only to warm thin gruel in a charred pot on a butane stove that Serena expected might explode any minute. The woman, her eyes slits, nodded to Serena and lay back down to doze again. "We're nomads!" she shouted, sitting up, eyes glassy with wonder, possibly talking while asleep. "Broke from the nursing home where they put us like meat to spoil and die. Free as birds." A snore escaped. "Free as birds," she murmured. And rolled over against her partner.

"Good for you," Serena said, wondering how they would make do in Tulsa. If they can do it, she thought, I can too. She had left everything behind except a small duffel of clothes and a one-person tent, a backpack with her pistol in it, and some keepsakes in the duffel to help remember Nana.

Good riddance to Fargo, she thought. So long, been good to know you. She said it with spite and venom, but her heart ached with desolation. Her stomach growled. The gruel disgusted her. Like eating warm toothpaste from a tube. She could smell manure, lots of it—was it the gruel?—and one of the girls up front made a *yuck-yuck* shout. She couldn't see much through the small opening, but it didn't take good eyes to understand thousands of heads of cattle crowded together in conditions that made her retch.

A concentration camp for cows, she thought. What would Nana say?

The stockyards were well guarded. The girls commented on the many rifles pointed their way as they drove past under dark skies. The caravan drivers kept in touch with phones and old walkie-talkies; there was lots of chatter until they passed the Militias. "Smell that shit? Whoo-ee!" "Keep your weapons cocked and loaded, everybody. Just in case. Easy does it." "Militia standing down by the roadside. Easy does it, folks."

The fecal odor receded. Wander and the other drivers relaxed. The sun came out. Quiet returned, just the sounds of the road, the tires *kalump*-ing, the wind finding its way into the van. Everybody carried a sheen of perspiration in the humidity like a second layer of skin until the air filled with dust, dry enough to tickle her nose and make her sneeze. Three times. She heard Nana. "Always sneeze three times. Twice for the saints and once for good luck."

She remembered *The Grapes of Wrath*, a book Nana had owned. Tom Joad, she thought. The Dust Bowl. California, here we come. If Tulsa doesn't work out. Where are you today, Tom Joad? "Among us, among us, among us," she heard Nana say, a chant Serena had long forgotten. She had traveled endless highways it seemed like forever with Nana, but they had never left the Dakotas or Minnesota.

The clouds, she remembered. Like mountains.

A sadness like a cold in the middle of summer; she could feel tears on one cheek. The van had bad shocks. Her stomach grumbled again. For some reason she imagined a boat tumbling about on high water. Please, Stomach, don't give me trouble, she pleaded, road weary, exhausted with anxiety when she thought about Tulsa, that bright dream of paradise fading into fog. Possible trouble in Tulsa—finding a room, finding work, staying safe, always the same shit—braided with images of Nana in hospice, dying in striped flannel jammies, sipping water, one sip at a time, sucking on slivers of ice, slipping into some other universe beyond Serena's ken, coming back alert to grip her hand in fright.

"Are you there?" she would say, eyes open but something wrong with her sight. The hospice workers, kind, professional, told her what to expect; it didn't help Nana. "Just be with her," one said, stroking Serena's hair, tied with a braid in back. "It matters."

The kind words didn't soften the blow when it came. It was a bright day. A hopeful day, Serena had thought, walking just after dawn to the hospice. Lots of light in the room. The stale, medicinal smells had been scrubbed away. A flicker of shadow on the white walls. No drama. The aroma of a bouquet of flowers she had brought with her. A spear of sunlight flashed into and through a

148

pitcher of drinking water. Low-cadenced voices in the hall. The clink of dishes and silverware. Strings of music someplace, a kind of waltz. Outside a big truck braked. Somebody shouted, irritated. The music stopped.

Nana breathed out, a sigh. Serena squeezed her hand with skin like rice paper and blue, collapsed veins. "The clouds are mountains," she said. A rasp. Serena stroked the still hand, a breath in. "Let's climb the clouds," she said. A moan, though barely audible. A rasp. Another breath out. A great sigh. Nana's face relaxed. And relaxed.

And didn't breathe back in.

Serena waited, holding her own breath. "Nana?"

She squeezed, hard. "Nana!"

* * *

Ava, in Tulsa, was in rehab. A minor mishap with heroin. Almost over now. The sweats gone, the pukes faded, the craving under control with methadone, though she promised herself she would kick that too, and soon. A few more days. Back on the wagon, once again a dear friend of Bill. Tess, her counselor, a woman with perpetually tangled ginger hair and a rigorous method but a tender smile, had helped her pull through.

The two of them shared a slice of chocolate cake.

"Sugar's good," Tess said.

"S-u-g-a-r," Ava said. Five letters. On a keyboard, four typed with the left hand, one with the right: That puts me ahead, 4–1. She did the math and pictured her fingers typing without really thinking about it. It was mild OCD, a strange new tic that came with sobriety—the number of letters, the keyboard, the contest between left and right hand, a winning hand announced in her head. If the left hand won, the goddess was placated; if the right, she felt bound to count another word. "Damn straight," she said, putting aside the mind clamor. "I had a diet once. No sugar. No carbohydrates."

Tess laughed, a pretty sound, and touched the dangling turquoise earring on one ear with slender fingers. "What kind of diet is that? And how did it go?"

"The wrong kind," Ava said. "It went bad. Believe you me. Supposed to clean me out."

"Ah," Tess said. "All kinds of crazy out there. You're too bony for that kind of diet. You need a diet that puts meat on your butt. Get yourself one of those Brazilian butt lifts."

They joked like that until Ava grew quiet. A thought struck her. "I came here," she said, "to find my daughter. Serena." This was an old story by now to Tess. "But you know what? Been so long I don't think I'd know her if I saw her."

Tess thought about that, chewed on cake. Ava wanted those earrings. E-a-r-r-i-n-g-s. Would Tess make them a gift to her if she asked? "She might know you." It was the kind of thing Tess said.

Ava didn't think it made sense. The first time they had this conversation, the withdrawal fogging everything, she had argued. "How the hell would you know? And why would she know me if I don't know her?" Tess had shrugged. Reassurance was the biscuit she offered. Now Ava had wised up, didn't argue, just nodded. "Maybe."

"Sure," Tess said. "Why don't you put some fliers around town with your phone number? *Looking for my daughter Serena. Information appreciated. Call this number.* Can't hurt. Include a picture. You can draw it yourself. From memory. Extrapolate. Make her look the way she might. Fliers help. And Craigslist. Can't go wrong there."

Was that a sarcasm? Ava acknowledged the attempt to help with a shrug. Therapy included painting, but not representational art. Would she be able to draw a face that looked real? She thought about it. Maybe. It had been a long time since she painted figures but, good or bad, it would fill the time until they gave her walking papers and helped her find a halfway house. Halfway room more like it, Ava thought, rueful. H-a-l-f-w-a-y. She would have to draw a self-portrait, though. How could she draw a young woman she hadn't seen for so many years?

* * *

The trailer park where Wander stopped was inside Tulsa, on the Arkansas River south of downtown. They were tested for the latest virus before the Police allowed them inside the city, but it would be a long walk to those Art Deco buildings she imagined she could see in the distance like the magic city of Oz. Wander checked into the park at a booth and backed into an open spot small enough for large vans, close to the public toilets and showers. Serena had just enough space outside the van to set up her tiny tent for the night. Wander didn't mind. The park manager—a wiry woman in khaki with a thousand smoker's wrinkles and short, cropped hair—folded her arms and squinted her eyes fiercely, as if affronted, at the tent when making the rounds but let it be when she spied Serena standing woebegone beside it.

Serena could only imagine what she looked like after days on the road without hygiene or decent rest. Her lower back ached when she tried to stand straight. She begged a few ibuprofen from Wander, who had a giant jar of pain pills that she dispersed like candy to her passengers. "All you have to do is ask," she said. Wander had lived on the road for years. It was her way of life. Serena felt sorry, though, for Man and Woman in the back of the van, though Wander was in no hurry to send them packing. There was room enough for Wander to sleep with the two of them, skinny as rails, sleeping to regather whatever strength they had left after eating the last of the thin gruel.

Goodbye to all that, Serena thought, what she thought too often when her Nana came to mind. She decided to thank Wander with a walk to the convenience store located at the park entrance to purchase a pack of hot dogs and some buns and a large cardboard urn of coffee.

* * *

Ava left the halfway house and stayed for weeks with Tess, in a storeroom attached to her garage that had a mattress on the floor. Tess helped her put an ad in Craigslist: *Hi. I'm looking for a room by the month to rent. Friend of Bill. Prefer female landlord.* Can't go wrong with Craigslist. Tess had meant it, although Ava also saw the effort as a message from Tess: Don't get too comfortable here. Tess also put her in touch with a recovery group. "Tulsa's not an expensive town," Tess said, pouring the two of them cups of boiling water over English Breakfast tea, "so long as you stay away from posh."

"But posh is my middle name," Ava said, tilting her head and blinking fast while pouting her lips.

It got the laugh she wanted. *I can make her laugh*, she thought. *It's been a long time.* Tess took a good, hard look at Ava's body.

What's this? Ava thought. Not that.

"You look about my size," she said. "Take off your shirt and jeans. Be right back." She left the room. Her cup of tea turned cold. Ava sat in her panties, taking deep conscious breaths and sipping her tea. She imagined herself in a diner painting by Edward Hopper. When she noticed that Tess's tea had turned cold, she nuked it in a small microwave over the stove and retrieved it just as Tess returned. "Thank you for that," Tess said. She carried an armful of clothes. "Old stuff," she said, "but still quality. Let's have a fashion show."

Ava modeled the clothes. Tess was right. They fit her like a glove. It might have been a lark, two girls having some fun, but Tess, sipping her nuked tea, stared at Ava as she posed and strutted as if the two of them were after a cure for cancer.

"They'll do," Tess said, still unsmiling.

Tess turned out to be a joker even in bed. The sex was pleasant, the aftermath less so. When Ava felt rage building and Tess started snoring up a storm, she thought about crawling off to sleep in the bath—the image an echo from some ancient song she could no longer remember—and instead gathered up her things, including the clothing from Tess and, to assuage her rage, the pair of turquoise earrings that Tess has placed inside a bedside drawer, and found her way to the mattress in the garage, where she surprised herself by sleeping like a stone until dawn.

* * *

Serena stood in the shower as long as she could before somebody shouted at her to get the hell done so somebody else could have a go. The hot water cleaned off the sweat and stink of the road but knocked her out. She crawled into her tent, put the duffel under her head, tucked the pack beside her as if cradling a lover to keep it safe, and went deaf and dumb for a good, long time. When she woke, it was midmorning.

Wander had a pot of coffee keeping warm on the propane burner placed on a card table with folding legs that she had set up outside like a lemonade stand. She motioned to Serena, who was groggy, and the two of them sat with coffee mugs and took in the sights. The two young women who had sat up front with Wander were gone. "One has a boyfriend here," Wander said. "They might or might not be back anytime soon." When Serena asked about the old couple, Wander pulled one of her ludicrous jet-black pigtails as if tugging on her brain pan with it and rolled her eyes. "God only knows. I've put out word around camp that they need something more permanent at their age than I can provide." She stared off into the middle distance; Serena followed her gaze but saw nothing except a cascade of vans, tents, and RVs, with stunted trees here and there. "Don't get me wrong," Wander said. "They've paid their way. Up-front. Social Security and something in the bank. I'm happy for it, but I'm no caretaker."

Serena was only half listening. "Huh," she said, hoping the grunt sounded commiserative. "I want to beat it today, go downtown, find a room if I can. You have any ideas?"

"You're welcome to stay a little while, get your bearings. If go you must"—the phrase sounded oddly formal to Serena—"there's still a bus route back and forth to town. You can catch it just down the road."

Serena finished the coffee, gave Wander a sincere hug—"See you down the road," Wander said—packed up and left. She could sense a spiral of depression like a cloud above her head. The day was overcast, promising rain. The trailer park depressed her, poor souls in bad shape trying to pretend otherwise. She had to beat it. Her fantasy of Tulsa was fading like the afterglow of a peyote high.

When the bus arrived, quiet and electric, better maintained than she expected, she was surprised that nobody inside wore a mask. But then she remembered that she had been tested. She relaxed. Tulsa was safe. Like Oz.

The bus stayed along the river for a while then turned into a neighborhood with gardens and an arboretum whose greenery almost seduced her into descending. She resisted the impulse and stayed aboard.

When in doubt, go.

* * *

When Ava finally made it to the kitchen, Tess was gone. There was a note on the fluted linoleum kitchen table. *Coffee in the pot, hon. Clean up, will you?* Ava shrugged, feeling an obligation, and drank coffee while she tidied up, scrubbing for Tess the way she had done for too many men. By the time she was done, she was *done*, too many scrubs and spit shines in her life, but the fridge was agleam, foodstuffs on the shelves rearranged by type, floor mopped on her hands and knees, soiled or dirty clothes—Tess, carefully attired on the job, was a slacker around her house—gathered and thrown in the wash. She drank coffee the whole while, mind racing, but stayed busy until she was done and had to think.

She didn't want to spend another night—the sex with Tess had left a sour taste in her body, which was listless on the methadone—but she knew that she wouldn't be capable of refusing her benefactor. She also understood how fragile she was, that a relapse could happen by impulse. And she wanted to draw that flier for Serena, get it photocopied, staple it on telephone poles and fence posts and bulletin boards.

She sipped coffee, a liquid lunch, thinking. She had an ache in one eye, a twinge that wouldn't stop. She still needed a buffer from life. She would stay put. The sex was only a price to pay. Besides, it was consensual. She couldn't remember complaining, except afterward, when Tess wanted certain things that Ava didn't particularly feel like doing.

Hell is other people, she remembered reading. That's all it is. I'm sick of them all.

Okay then. She sent Tess a text asking her to purchase a sketch pad and colored pencils. *Will pay you back*, she wrote, to keep a shred of self-respect. She held the turquoise earrings in the palm of one hand, admiring them, what the light did inside the sky-blue and greenish stones, the glint of the silver settings. She put them back, regretfully but righteously, where they belonged. Besides, the inexplicable rage that had incited the theft was gone.

She was wiped out. She had a headache that wouldn't quit and felt her insides rumble, an incitement to riot. She knew that she could have methadone. Not, she decided, and returned to the mattress with its thin sheet and ratty blanket in the garage to imagine what Serena might look like all these years later. It was a zero-sum game she played: She couldn't have the methadone if she wanted Serena. She wanted to find her daughter; therefore, she had to sweat out the poison.

Get back to the garden, she thought. G-a-r-d-e-n. Left hand, 5; right hand, 1.

* * *

Tulsa is paradise, Serena snickered. *What was I thinking?* She could feel her day shaping up as a senseless lump of clay. On the way downtown, she spied small gatherings of people out in the streets but stayed on the bus until it reached something called Cathedral Square and a street sign that declared the square bordered Historic Route 66. She descended from the bus with her gear and stood across from a stone fortress that she realized was a church near another smaller building with a dome on top. She wandered about the deserted streets past a posh place called the Petroleum Club. Oil, even now, was big in Tulsa, she remembered. There were several churches with steeples. There had been plenty of God-haunted folk in Fargo, and now she realized she was smackdab in the middle of the Bible Belt.

She despised religion but liked good deeds. I can be a Christian, she thought, if it means a hot meal and a cot. She realized she wasn't in the part of town where she would find homeless shelters. Where were all the people, the festivity and fantasy, the carnivalesque utopia that was Tulsa?

Her stomach grumbled. More bullshit. That's what it was.

She walked a mile or so, made a note when she passed an employment center, noted a large arena as a landmark, and wandered into a rundown part of town, the wrong side apparently, where a woman in jeans and a bomber jacket walking a big, mangy dog directed her to a building with a big sign out front that read "Need Help Getting Back on Your Feet?"

A pale man with big ears in a funny, makeshift church collar brought her into his office, gave her a cup of coffee, and told her she could return at dusk for dinner and a cot. The place was called the Lost and Found Ministry. He took down her name to save her a place—no ID needed—and even let her leave her duffel with the tent attached in a closet in one corner of the large room that smelled of mildew. The room had a wooden desk with its white paint peeling and piles of old clothing and shit that he acknowledged with a wave of his hand. "Yours for the taking," he said. "Anything you need?"

Serena felt an irrational urge to kick him in the balls and felt her face flush with embarrassment at the impulse. She wiped her forehead of sweat. She must look a mess. "Thank you," she said, though saying the words was difficult. "No thank you. Just a meal and a place to sleep."

"My name's Heimlich," he said. "But most people call me Weezie." He struck a pose as if on stage. The fooling around made her see him differently, as a personality and not a functionary. Her mood changed; she laughed and meant it. His pose was a gesture meant to put her at ease, she could tell; she realized her anger had nothing to do with him. He was kind, generous. It was the old clothes; they had brought her Nana to mind.

She was enraged that her Nana was gone. She wanted to kick the world in the balls, she realized, and any substitute at hand would do.

She smiled his way, though not at him. He took it like that, though, and appeared to be pleased. "I appreciate the help," she said, meaning it.

He nodded. "A warning," he said. "We're using potatoes as protein in dinner tonight, I'm sorry to say. That's just the way it is. If you want something with more meat on its bones, you had better eat it out there." He stared at her, a finger to his chin, as if sizing her up. "You know, we need somebody to help out, keep the place clean. Room and board and chump change." He tilted his head and opened wide his face, raising his hands as a question mark.

"Huh," she said. "Can I chew on it?"

"Sure thing. Have a good one." Weezie—the name was growing on her—reached down for a sheaf of papers and turned away from her to a filing cabinet.

* * *

It took Ava almost a week to get her bearings. Tess continued to be helpful and kind. The sex wasn't any kind of demand. Rather, Tess made it clear that a bed partner was welcome on Ava's own terms and left it at that. The two became companionable. Ava withstood her cravings and nauseas, drank plenty of liquids, ate mostly soup and salad, used the toilet as a porcelain throne when needed, and did housework with a vengeance. She found herself counting letters in words less frequently.

She drew a portrait of herself in charcoal, a snapshot of her taken by Tess, and a drawing of Serena as a young child and a young adult— as she imagined her—with colored pencil. Tess thought it came out good, and took the final draft to work with her on a Friday to photocopy. "I'll staple some to utility poles," she said, "and you can take it this weekend from there."

Only problem: Reality was flat, two-dimensional, gray. Nothing much mattered. She tried to care but found herself not giving a crap.

158

About anything. She knew it was process, part of the cure, or whatever a clinician might call it, the serotonin balancing out dopamine; but knowing something, even in her visionary moments, never did much good.

Maybe she was due for a change.

* * *

In Fargo, all roads lead to Tulsa. Lots of people said it, some with passion; some, Serena now realized, with sarcasm. She had such high hopes crossing the prairie, the plains, the mountains, sparse desertlike terrain, sagebrush and tumbleweed, crops and cattle.

Tulsa was a shithole. She should have stayed with the nomads, maybe followed their lead—rebuilt an old truck into a living space, lived everywhere and nowhere, found seasonal work.

Instead, this: The Woody Guthrie and Bob Dylan Centers were closed until further notice, Cain's had a padlock on its door and an empty calendar. Downtown, the Art Deco buildings were elaborate and worth her time as eye candy but closed off to people like her. She knew there were people worth finding; that the rumors were bound to mean something; that she could find friends, a place to stay, a job; but the heart inside her felt like it might die. Wherever you go, she thought, there you are.

She had expected the streets to be full of vendors, groups of celebrants, cowboys and itinerants, singers and good cops, men her age to flirt with and kiss. Where was everybody?

There were restaurants near Woody Guthrie's place, a few open for business, so she had jerk chicken and a salad with fried okra in it. The waitress, with a Jamaican accent, was kind. While she ate, she browsed a battered large paperback anthology, *Visiting Bob: Poems Inspired by the Life and Work of Bob Dylan*, with a photo of a very young Bob Dylan on its cover sitting at a piano in what must have been his house at the time, surrounded by blankets and books and knickknacks. The thought of him made her cry because it reminded her of her Nana, who had often listened to his music as they drove without a destination.

After the meal, standing outside on the street, Serena felt like she could sleep for a week. She headed back for the Lost and Found Ministry. She would find them, the people who could matter to her.

* * *

Ava spent the weekend stapling fliers wherever she could around the parts of town where she figured Serena, if she came to Tulsa, might hang out. Bulletin boards in coffee shops and shelters and community centers. Employment centers and temp job agencies. Restaurants where food was cheap. The library. Without a recent photo, there was no point in asking strangers if they had seen a young woman she couldn't describe. "Somebody who looks like me, only not so strung out." Yeah, that would help. That would do the trick.

She sat on a wooden bench facing an empty lot to catch her breath. Tulsa is a broken world, she thought, like everyplace else. It's a broken world.

As she sat, one finger playing with a splinter, she was so tired in her bones, all she could think about was crawling back to her mattress.

The clouds opened and a dull facsimile of a sun made its first appearance. She felt turned topsy-turvy, as if the clouds were underfoot and the leaden earth above her.

Ava's phone wasn't smart. She realized she needed the internet, though she and Tess had already tried finding Serena that way. She stood in a rush and felt faint, had to sit again and rise carefully with one hand on the back of the bench. And breathe, but she had a plan:

Get back to base station, nap, hydrate, fire up the laptop Tess said she could use. It was a plan. Not much of one, but it would have to do until she found something better.

* * *

Serena served dinner to dozens who stood in line waiting for a place at the feast. Though Weezie had joked that potatoes were the meal's protein, the stew they served had all sorts of things in it that smelled good and tasted better. It worked like that every day. Many of the faces at table appeared as forlorn and worn down as the ones she had once studied in a book called *Let Us Now Praise Famous Men*, with photographs by Walker Evans that brought to mind the songs of Woody Guthrie. One family of five bowed their heads in prayer, their clothes so tattered and dusty that Steinbeck's *Grapes of Wrath* came again to mind. "Thank you for the soup kitchen meal," their wrinkled and emaciated patriarch, a tiny man who looked like Charles Manson but had kind eyes, said to her when she stopped to greet the family.

"This is what I call a Grand Food Hall," she answered, "but we do sometimes serve soup. You're welcome anytime."

In the middle of the meal service, Weezie had to motion to a big, burly biker in a sleeveless leather vest and hair pulled back in a braid to escort a troublemaker from the dining room. He was shouting at an Asian woman in a wheelchair who appeared to have dementia because her eyes were like saucers and her mouth hung open in what Serena took to be either shock or derangement. The troublemaker, his face contorted in rage, screamed out obscenities; he wore a long, greasy suede coat, even though it was humid and hot inside the hall, and the biker grabbed him quick from behind when he reached under it as if going for a gun.

The biker, with assistance from two other diners, roughly escorted the guy from the hall. Serena heard him continue to shout: "You fuckers! I'll be back, you fascist fucks!"

Otherwise, everybody who came to eat was grateful, their eyes haunted by loneliness and homelessness. Most people, when they get fed, feel good. Serena thought of Ava, who was no doubt dead or so far gone on pills and meth and synthetic junk that she might be better off dead. She shook her head fiercely to clear it. If she stayed employed at the Lost and Found Ministry, one day Ava might walk in the door and stand in line for a hot meal. She had to admit that these were her kind of people, that she herself was homeless.

Tulsa, she thought, blowing out a sigh as if filling a balloon with air.

When she complained after cleanup to Weezie that the town was shut down, he made a face. "Some of that shit is seasonal," he said. "That Dylan place opens when it wants to. You a fan?"

"My Nana was a big fan. Maybe the biggest. I think of her when I hear him sing."

Weezie nodded with sympathy. The two had already become friends; he often invited her to sit for coffee with him in his office. He had lived for a time in Fargo and knew the place inside out. He talked about The Riots as if they were an everyday occurrence there, but the city had been peaceful enough, especially in winter, which kept the riffraff out.

"Only two seasons in Fargo," he said. And winked. It was a very old joke.

"Yeah, I know. Winter. And road construction. Not so much of that these days."

He liked to call himself President Weezie. "You're my chief of staff," he said, making it clear that she could take her good time finding a more permanent place to lay her head. "When I think of Dylan," he said, shaking his head, "I think of a beautiful turd. If I was Bob Dylan, I would laminate it, frame it, title it, and put it on a gallery wall in London; his estate could include outtakes in one of his bootleg albums."

Serena stared at him.

"I mean," Weezie said, "he's been dead for how many years? You know the urn with his ashes is on display in that museum? And yet new bootlegs come out every damn year. Did he ever sing a note without recording it?" Serena was glaring at him. He shrugged and held out a hand. "No offense to your Nana; I'm kind of kidding around, one Fargoan to another?" he said. "Anyway, Cain's a different story. They're open every Sunday afternoon for a big shindig. Music, dance, jams. We can go this Sunday if you'd like."

She laughed. "You mean a date, Weezie?"

His big ears turned red. "I'll dude myself up," he said. "You do the same." Her glare again. "Or not. Doesn't matter. People come and go any which way." He pointed a finger. "What do you say?" He froze like a mime with his odd face and big red ears cocked as if listening for a sound he would never hear.

"Sure," she said. "Cool. I'm in." She was touched when he made it clear she was welcome to live and work at the nonprofit for as long as she wished, but she wanted her own place—a house or even an apartment, however narrow and tight, with a window that had a lightweight, bright-colored curtain for privacy. Books, an old comfortable couch free of bugs or lice, food in the fridge. A bottle of cheap wine open on a table with a bright yellow tablecloth. And a special friend she could invite at her leisure to visit.

That wasn't much to ask, was it? To find somebody to build a house with?

"I have some paper to file," Weezie said brusquely. "Can you clean up the bulletin board out front, make sure it's all up to date?"

"Sure." She stared at him. "You all right? We all right?"

He grinned. "Yes," he said. He nodded. "One must fasten one's gaze. That's all."

* * *

"Watch for a parking spot," Tess said. They were downtown, in the Arts District near Cain's, and Tess wore a fashionable sheath in black and gold complemented by silver shoes with heels.

Ava laughed. "We're fashion boats," she said. It was her first real outing since her relapse.

"It's social hour on Sundays at Cain's," Tess said. "Everybody who's anybody shows up. Be my date. Behave yourself."

The comment irked Ava. "There," she said, pointing. Tess swerved, drawing an irritated blast from somebody's horn, but then took her time to inch back and forth into the parking spot. "If I wasn't so brain-dead, I'd do it for you," Ava said. "I'm a parallel parker nonpareil. First-place finish in the parallel parking Olympics." She felt all right. She was in tight jeans and a long-sleeved black lamé pullover tee that had the word "lamé" embossed on the front.

The clothes, of course, had come from Tess, and Ava, studying herself in the bedroom mirror, had wondered, keeping her voice idle like a car engine in neutral, if Tess would mind lending her the turquoise earrings to go with the outfit. T-u-r-q-u-o-i-s-e. Left hand, 5; right hand, 4.

"The earrings suit you," Tess now said, the two of them crossing the street to Cain's, where a shaggy-haired man with a painted guitar slung over one shoulder was gabbing with another man in a speckled sports coat and tie holding a sax above his waist as if he might stop at the entryway and play tunes for spare change. The wind was high, and Ava felt free for the first time in weeks. She'd taken the cure. It's getting me through, she thought.

Inside, Tess spied a friend—a dude with a ten-gallon hat and Western shirt with metal buttons who gave her a hug, whistled appreciatively at the both of them, even winked, and took Tess aside to chat her up about something that sounded like business, but not before asking them both what they were drinking. "Chardonnay," Tess said.

"The same," Ava said.

Tess gave her a look with lips stretched and a slight shake of the head but left it at that. There was a wooden stage on the near side of the long room where musicians gathered and a bar at the far end with stools. Ava studied the sparse crowd, though it was increasing by the minute, until Tess tapped her on a shoulder with a glass of fizzy liquid. "I hope you don't mind," she said. "I switched it for ginger ale."

Ava did mind. Very much. She wanted a drink. Bad. She felt good. A vodka tonic would be just what the doctor ordered. Chardonnay had been her compromise.

Tess was still her counselor, though, if also landlady and lover, so she nodded and sipped the fizz without complaint. "You're a functioning adult," Tess added, making Ava squirm: TMI. "I'm not taking that away. I just didn't know what to do, off the cuff. If you want the wine, I'll fetch it."

Ava squinched up her face. "I'm fine," she said. She wasn't. Every muscle in her body tightened. She wanted more than a drink. D-r-i-n-k. Right hand wins, 3–2. A-p-p-e-t-i-t-e. Left hand wins, 5–3. She recalled something from television, a game show, *Wheel of Fortune.* Spin the giant wheel, pick a letter, spin again if the letter can be found on the board.

She wasn't sure how long she lost herself in the fugue state. When she became aware again of where and who she was, she was bare-handed, her empty glass of ginger ale—had she been so thirsty?—placed on a nearby table. Several musicians on stage were playing bluegrass. "I'm Working on a Building." She wagged her head in time to the rhythm. R-h-y-t-h-m. Left hand loses, 4–2.

Somebody said something to her. Ava heard the sentence but was so deep inside her head, it didn't compute.

* * *

Serena said it again. "Excuse me. Are you my mother? Ava?"

The woman in a glittering blouse had fingers that jittered as if she had a case of palsy. Serena had a copy of the flier, taken from the bulletin board at the Lost and Found Ministry. In her other hand she held a bottle of beer she drank down fast, too fast. She almost choked on it. She finished it, coughed, put it aside.

The woman's blue eyes pierced like cut glass.

"Are you my mother?" Serena felt tears coming.

The woman moistened her lips and moved her mouth as if trying to speak. Her eyes darted everyplace they could except on Serena.

"Ava? You Ava? The palindrome?"

The woman squinted as if there was too much light in the room.

"You're my mother? Ava?" Serena waved the flier. "This is yours?"

The bluegrass band close at hand reached its crescendo. The singer, with a mess of dark curls, played his mouth harp for all he was worth. Serena saw the woman's hands jitter, as if counting the bars of music or the hours or the days. She stared into the glassy eyes, the bluest ones she'd ever seen.

* * *

S-e-r-e-n-a. Six letters. Left hand, 4; right hand, 2. No. That's not right: 5–1.

Ava felt vertigo. The earth tilted at a steep angle. She could fall right off if she let go. The dancehall filled with clouds and cloven earth, the clouds beneath her again, the earth above. She could hear a high thin mercury sound like quicksilver that had nothing to do with the bluegrass music on stage.

166

No philosophy. No history. No medicine. No tomorrow. Just today. This moment.

S-e-r-e-n-a. Six letters.

* * *

"Don't you hear me? Did you make this flier? Are you my mother?" Serena felt a high, whining panic build in her chest. She squinted for signs of Nana in the gaunt woman's face. She felt a crazy urge to tear into the woman like a bulldog and either punch in her face or cling and cry.

The woman stared at her, from inside a cave, deaf and dumb. Her lips rubbed together, tongue flicking as if her mouth was gummy and needed more saliva before words might emerge.

The high, keening sound in the air felt wild enough to rupture her eardrums. Where was it coming from?

"Are you Ava? Are you my mother?"

Say *yes*. Please.

Ava flinched, took a step back, dazed, her arms folded across her chest.

Serena reached out on autopilot, hypnotized, the unfolding moment overlapping with her imagination, her outstretched fingers almost steady, as if seized by electrical current. One must fasten one's gaze, she thought.

Ava, against her will, a changeling who only resembled the woman she had once been, touched Serena's fingertips with her own, felt a spark, as if by touch she could summon a part of herself that was lost forever and could never be found.

Words didn't come, but she nodded, stared into her daughter's eyes—*my daughter*, she thought—felt muscles in her neck strain and struggle.

She swam against a wild sea where many bodies were buried.

Acknowledgments

I want to thank my companions who've stayed stubborn and loyal to their creativity and inspiration in a world gone sometimes drastically wrong. I especially want to thank those writers and friends, both near and far away, who offered suggestions and advice. I would be very lonely without them. Only connect, and celebrate moments of happiness, joy and contentment as we all quickly age on a planet orbiting around its sun at about 67,000 mph. Think of that simple calculation and take a look at the sky on a clear night if your sense of wonder ebbs.

I also especially want to thank Chris Madden, David LeGere, Miranda Heyman, LJ Mucci, Paulette Baker, and everyone at Woodhall Press who worked with me on Clouds Are the Mountains of the World.

About the Author

Alan Davis grew up in Louisiana near the mouth of the Mississippi. *So Bravely Vegetative* won the Prize Americana for Fiction; *Alone with the Owl* and *Rumors from the Lost World* won the Many Voices Project Competition. He's co-editor of *Visiting Bob: Poems Inspired by the Life and Work of Bob Dylan* and of ten editions of *American Fiction: The Best Unpublished Short Stories by Emerging Writers*, chosen by *Writer's Digest* during his tenure as one of the top fifteen places to publish fiction in the United States. He has received a Loft-McKnight Award of Distinction in Creative Prose, a Minnesota State Arts Board Fellowship, a Fulbright to Slovenia, and a Fulbright-Hays Grant to Indonesia. He served as editor of New Rivers Press, an independent press founded in 1968, from 2001–2016 after helping to relocate it to Minnesota State University, where it continued to publish titles in all genres and served as a teaching press to prepare students for careers in publishing. He's professor emeritus at Minnesota State University and has also taught at the University of North Carolina and in low-residency master of fine arts (MFA) programs in Maine (Stonecoast) and Connecticut (Fairfield University). He lives in Minnesota, near the Mississippi's headwaters.